Happy Reading

new friend, Mary.

Phyllis Muller

She's Gotta Be Kiddin'!

Justa Housewife?

by

Phyllis Miller

Bloomington, IN

Milton Keynes, UK

AuthorHouse™
1663 Liberty Drive, Suite 200
Bloomington, IN 47403
www.authorhouse.com
Phone: 1-800-839-8640

AuthorHouse™ UK Ltd.
500 Avebury Boulevard
Central Milton Keynes, MK9 2BE
www.authorhouse.co.uk
Phone: 08001974150

First published by AuthorHouse 11/29/2006

ISBN: 978-1-4259-6420-7 (sc)

Library of Congress Control Number: 2006908282

Printed in the United States of America
Bloomington, Indiana

This book is printed on acid-free paper.

ACKNOWLEDGEMENTS

A special thank you to all those helped in the preparation of this book. This includes family, friends, teachers, and even strangers who wrote to compliment me on something I had written. I hesitate to name names, for I would surely miss someone. Enough people said, "You should write a book about that" to encourage me to accept the challenge.

Our son, Wes, before he died, would drop in with a smile, a hug and some flowers and allow me privacy at my keyboard. Our daughter, Laurie, did a final, but quick edit of the galley to save her mother from embarrassment over some careless mistake. My husband, Jim, stayed loyal and patient during my long stint on the job.

The young folks at Author House very patiently and pleasantly took care of the technical part.

PROLOGUE

I knew that I had to write this book after a dinner table conversation one evening when a contemporary of mine was asked if she had worked. Others at the table were of the Baby Boomer age and had spoken of their profitable careers, but this lady said, "Naw, I was just a haus frau." I said, "And just what did you do?" Suddenly her eyes grew large. Her mouth opened, and with just a little prodding out poured words after words about chore after chore. She started with laundering and ironing five white shirts a day for her husband and children who attended private schools. Then she said that she not only organizes everything, but plans meals, shops, cooks, does dishes, washes, irons, mends, sews, knits, drives, tutors, advises, comforts, has PTA, Boy Scouts, and church meetings. She could have gone on all night, but I said, "Please don't use that term, "just a housewife" in my presence ever again." She shrugged. That was the job life had assigned to her, and she had done it well.

That is fine if she is appreciated. In my opinion she is a homemaker and as such is a very important person. Without her the rest of the family could not have their successes. We know one dear widower who has commented about his loneliness after the loss of two good wives and the fact that he doesn't have anyone to tell him what to do or how to do it. Females have filled that roll for men for years. Yes, I've always done those things. But it wasn't until a year after Justa was born that women were even allowed to vote. I don't say that they were GIVEN the vote, because they worked hard for it and were beaten up for it. I recently read a book published in 1890 that was found hidden in the walls of a plantation house. Some female had the nerve to read it but had to hide it from the men in the house. The problem was that it pointed out in a very clever way that the men took credit for a lot of the work that the women did.

Justa thinks that the problem brought out by Betty Friedan's "Feminine Mystique" in 1963 is still there for many women. She described it as "the unhappiness of post World War II women unfulfilled by traditional notions of female domesticity." Justa's dinner partner indicated that by saying "I was just a haus frau". It would have been better if she had been able to reply proudly, "I'm the chief executive officer of the home front and the guidance counselor for the whole family." The proper terminology might solve the whole problem.

"A hundred men may make an encampment, but it takes a woman to make a home."

— A Chinese proverb

CONTENTS

65 YEARS WITH THE SAME MAN? HOW DID SHE DO IT?

It was Justa and Jim's 65th wedding anniversary. She was told by a friend, "You shouldn't be running around like this. There are sick people and germs." Justa replied, "I'm not running to catch the germs. I'm running away from them. "She was also asked, "Where do you get the energy to do all these things?" Justa replied, "I just do these things, and that gives me energy." You always look so happy, and yet you've had so much heartache." She answers, "Because of the adversity, I appreciate more the happy days. One needs some rain in order to recognize the sunshine." When people ask her, "How could you ever live with one person all those years?" Justa jokingly replies, "Because he tricked me. That's how. Right from the beginning that's what he did." On the honeymoon that first night, he had reservations at the Palmer House in Chicago. It was the lovely bridal suite with flowers and all. He had planned everything perfectly just as she and her mother did the wedding.

Beautiful formal wedding April 12, 1941

But something was not quite right. The pastor had said, "Who giveth this woman?" Not "Who giveth this man?" That was inequality right from the start. She did insist that her Dad say, "Her mother and I do." She was giving up her name and her career opportunities. In those days women seldom worked away from the house with a paying job if a good man had proposed to her and promised to love and care for her forever more. In most cases that gave the man the power because he had the purse strings. She always tried to do things his way. He loved her and couldn't deny her anything she wanted. Therefore it worked. The children took their father's name. Equality would have been half of his name and half of hers. If Miss Spalding married Mr. Miller, the children could take a last name of Spalder or Milling. Well, it's just a thought. From day one she put his towels up first on the left and hers second on the right. That also worked with toothbrushes; so when in a hotel or visiting family, there was no confusion. His was left. She was right. Well, you see she wanted to be sure that she was right on something. But to be honest with you there was more to it than that.

On that first day of marriage they left the Palmer House in Chicago and started their drive to the Smoky Mountains. Jim had made reservations for the week. They stopped in Pekin, Illinois for lunch. That was nice, but after they had driven about 50 miles out of town, Justa realized that she had left her purse with all their gift money in it at the restaurant. This was a good chance for Jim to show his lack of control and anger at her carelessness. That's what I mean about his being sneaky. He simply smiled at her, turned the car around, and drove the 50 miles back. As they opened the restaurant door a young lady reached under the counter, took out the purse and handed it to Justa. Everything was intact, and they were once again on their way to the mountains.

It's a little hard to fight with a man like that especially when she knew that she hadn't exactly delighted him on their first night together. Or maybe she had. Instead of a sexy gown, she had been sold an attractive pair of pajamas that were really meant to be a maturity outfit that would open out to allow for a baby in there too. It would be a little difficult to put a baby in there when she didn't really understand how that was to be accomplished. She'd had absolutely no experience, and he was patient.

He continued this behavior. I will tell you that he had saved enough money to rent a nice apartment. He had enough to buy all new furniture that they picked out together. They had many friends and showers and a big formal wedding; so the gifts made quite a fine home. He helped with everything. How could she possibly not be kind to him? She gave him one more opportunity. The final straw should have come when she unpacked cosmetics and put a bottle of bright red nail polish on the top shelf of a bathroom cabinet. That was a dumb move. In some way it managed to fly off and crash to the newly tiled floor. Red nail polish splashed everywhere. If this wasn't a chance to scream, I don't know what is. He was in love, yes, but this was not normal. He was on his hands and knees cleaning up the mess. She was trapped. If he was going to be so kind and decent, what choice did she have? She had to be nice to him too. Sneaky, but wonderful. She never regretted it.

HE WAS SUCCESSUL AND THERE WERE PERKS

Jim was the executive-vice president of the Chuckles Candy Co. (later a subsidiary of Nabisco). At that time Chuckles jelly candies were advertised as "five colors, five flavors, five cents." Some people assumed that that was a really "sweet" job. His office was up front, but Justa knew that he made constant forays back into the factory. She teasingly accused him of simply being the chief candy taster. He started as comptroller but advanced quickly. He managed the company. He also negotiated contracts with the union. He was a wonderful employer, because he was honest, kind, considerate and hard working. He had an excellent secretary, Helen Skoog, who kept him in line at the office and who went back to their home to retrieve keys or whatever paper he might have failed to take to work. Justa was at the other end supplying his needs. There were other wonderful employees.

Legislation to apply the principle of equal pay for equal work without discrimination because of sex is a matter of simple justice.

—Dwight D. Eisenhower

There were perks that came to him for his work. She would be unfair not to admit how many of those came to her because of Jim. It was done in the name of friendship, but that was because of his job. A private jet picked them up to go to New York for a candy convention. Their daughter, Laurie, was included. It was on that plane ride that she learned to play gin rummy with the men. They stayed at the Waldorf Astoria. At dinnertime a table was reserved on the dance floor. When Jim and Justa got up to dance, Paul Anka went to the table and sang to Laurie. While they were still on the floor, the waiter brought a large plate of oysters on the half shell to their daughter. They saw her gorgeous large eyes double in size. Well, not exactly, but she was obviously impressed.

They made it a habit of going to New York City yearly in November just to get caught up on all the plays. A business associate by the name of Hirsh learned of their first trip. He and his wife had a beautiful residence on Park Avenue. They offered to show Justa and Jim around the city. They ended up basically adopting "those kids" for that week and showed them all over the city. Each time that they made the trip, the Hirshes showed them everything there was to see. They were delighted to take tours to places that they themselves had never visited. Both couples enjoyed the friendship.

Other treats included sail boating on Lake Michigan and personal tours in Boston. One of her biggest jobs was at Christmas time when there were so many gifts that were duplicates and needed to be shared with others—fruit cakes, turkeys, hams, fruit boxes, Chanel #5, and a special university gift each year from its president. This was all very nice, and, of course, Justa wrote thank you notes and reciprocated when possible.

She was always thrilled when they received a certificate for live Maine lobster for ten, bibs and all included. She'd throw a party. Everybody wanted that invitation. One year she was ill, possibly because of all this work in addition to a full schedule. She put the certificate in a file cabinet. It was several years later when she saw it again. Jim said, "That's too bad." She didn't think so. She called the lobster business to ask if it was too late. It wasn't!

DANVILLE FRIENDS SIMILAR SITUATIONS

Because of his work, the friends that they made in Danville, Illinois were those who had comparable positions. That meant their wives also had similar responsibilities. There were about eight couples that were best friends for years. Husbands and wives served as chairpersons or on committees for all the charitable work in the community whether it was a fundraiser, the Salvation Army, the Red Cross, the church, country club, or the symphony ad infinitum.

THEY HELPED EACH OTHER

When she led the Spring Lakes Council of (condominium) Associations for seven years, he supported her all the way and was the one person always relied on to audit the books. When he was president of the Sarasota Area Northwestern University Club for four years and then as became a Regent, they both served on that board and attended together the yearly leadership conferences in Evanston, Illinois. When Jim was chosen as one of the outstanding alumni of Northwestern, there was a big dinner party for all of those chosen. Another honoree was the head of Motorola. Justa spent the evening talking to his father who had previously held that position. She has always been as comfortable talking to the C.E.O. as anyone with any position, in any land, in any tongue. She started that as a young child when she went around the neighborhood chatting with all the adults. They called her "Little Miss Sunshine". She continued to think that's who she was as she kept walking, talking and smiling. I'd better back up a bit and start at the beginning. It will make it easier to understand her.

OUT OF THE WOMB AND INTO THE WORLD

It was January 12, 1918 in Elgin, Illinois when Justa decided that she was ready to leave the womb. A severe snowstorm made streets, driveways, and sidewalks right up to the front door completely inaccessible. No one could get to a doctor or hospital, and no one could get to their house. There was only one solution as John saw it although it appeared to be an almost impossible task. He would take his wide snow shovel and clear the five blocks to Sherman Hospital. He dressed warmly and helped his pretty, very pregnant little wife into a warm coat, hat, mittens, and boots. She would walk directly behind him in his footprints. It would be difficult, but that was their only choice. They knew that anything worthwhile was seldom easy. Laura had given birth to one healthy son but had lost one and didn't want to lose another. Their daughter-to-be was already making it clear that she had a mind of her own. She was kicking up a storm. She wanted out, and when she wanted something, she wanted it yesterday. However, once the walk started and Justa was getting some fresh air she decided that her parents finally realized that she wouldn't wait much longer. She calmed down a little.

Justa and Jim are always complimented on how beautifully they dance together. When asked when she started dancing, Justa replies, "As soon as I popped out of the womb." Perhaps she was practicing her steps on that walk before birth. She arrived with all the appropriate fingers and toes. Friends and relatives coming to inspect the new arrival all made the usual and expected comments about the lovely baby. When Justa was young, she heard these stories but also that Laura's sister, Evelyn, observed the newcomer and said, "Thank goodness the baby doesn't have a nose like John's." The first time the baby looked in the mirror and understood those words, she realized in fact that she did have a nose exactly like John's. This troubled Justa for years. In a classroom if she thought that someone was staring at her, she would hold a book or paper up to conceal her profile. Although she was often told that she was beautiful, she knew she was funny looking because she had a nose like John's. It didn't matter that people always said he was handsome. She recently met a woman who knew nothing of Justa's problem but was always concerned about HER nose. Her mother had said it always turned beautiful when she put a smile under it. Justa has always smiled, but she didn't know if that could make her beautiful.

Babies are such a nice way to start people.

— Don Herold

HER FIRST BEST FRIEND WAS BARBARA

Barbara with Courier News Doll

Before starting school Justa's best friend was Barbara. That family was so good to her. They were well to do, but that didn't mean anything to Justa except she was impressed with their big sleeping porch. When they invited her to dinner she was served as a young lady. The crystal was so fine that one evening Justa literally took a bite out of the goblet. They just took it in stride. The German maid, Gertrude, brought another glass, and Justa wasn't made to feel the least embarrassed. Sometimes the girls set up a lemonade stand. Gertrude fixed the drinks, but the girls sold it and then gave the income to a needy organization. They got some good sales experience and an idea of charity.

Barbara's aunt and uncle were very wealthy. When the girls took elocution lessons or dancing lessons, Barbara's Aunt Birdy sent her limo to take the girls. There was a chauffeur and footman dressed in gray livery. The footman got out and opened the door for the little ladies. Barbara always let Justa play with her beautiful BIG Courier News doll. When her aunt traveled to Paris, she brought special felt Parisian dolls to both girls. Justa still had hers when they moved to the retirement home in 2003. On that final "downsizing" in Florida she sold the remains of her collection of 500 dolls. She had beautiful porcelain antique ones but also some poorer quality dolls that had been abused that she had rejuvenated and redressed. At the end she did keep her favorite, the one she had "mothered" and played with so much as a child. It still sits in the child's rocker that had belonged to her father. As a teenager she was shown this antique chair. Nobody really wanted to fuss with it. It had come apart and needed to be re-glued. It needed stripping and refinishing. Justa did all that and then she had an experienced individual cane it. That special doll still sits in that special chair to greet visitors to their home.

BARBARA MISTREATED BECAUSE SHE WAS JEWISH

One day when the two were quite young several older children walked by, picked up Barbara and carried her out and put her down in the middle of the street. Justa didn't understand why. That was dangerous. Justa helped her friend get back into the yard. As an adult Justa realized that it was only because her friend was Jewish that she was treated so horribly. When Justa started work on this book, she tracked down Barbara to tell her how much Barbara and her family had meant to her. Before she could speak, Barbara said, "What I remember most is that I fell, hurt my head, your Dad put me on his shoulders and carried me to the hospital."

SCHOOL 1924-1932

She knew that the Declaration of Independence said that, "All men are created equal". Perhaps what it meant was "all white men". It didn't say, "all people black, white, male, or female". In grade school when she questioned the teacher on why books used only the words "he" or "him", she was told that that included girls as well as boys. Justa didn't think that that should be. They just pretended that to be so. Why were females in a different category? Would the boys like it if they were told that when they used "she or "her", that included the male? When she saw that the boys were able to use the gym every day for basketball, but the girls had very little time to practice captain ball, she did something about it. She was a friendly little girl who visited with the neighbors. One of them happened to be Miss Gillihan who was the principal of the school. Justa told her how she felt about this. The principal was a smart lady who recognized the inequity and replied, "You've got it. You'll have equal time." To the surprise and delight of all except possibly the basketball team, the girls won the city championship. That huge first place banner hung high on the wall above the steps for years at McKinley School in Elgin.

GRADE SCHOOL TEACHERS TAUGHT MORE THAN SUBJECT

Her first grade teacher made her think that arithmetic was a game. Miss Norton mimeographed sheets of addition, subtraction, multiplication and fractions. Pupils would get one sheet placed face down on their desks. When Miss Norton gave the "go" signal, they started. When that sheet was finished, they could go to the front desk for the next sheet and continue solving until time was up. It was fun. The winner was the first one who had the most sheets done correctly. Justa could win because she loved doing it. She ended up majoring in math and later used that in teaching electronics for the Army Air Force in World War II.

Miss Baker was her second grade teacher and had the most beautiful penmanship. She wrote in purple ink and taught her pupils how to write this way. Justa's mother framed the Palmer penmanship certificate that she received and had it on the wall for years as though it was a really fine accomplishment. However, as they got older and had to take notes and think fast, the writing deteriorated severely. But she never lost the memory of how very elegant penmanship could be if the writer just slowed down. Now they can use a tape recorder or scribble their notes, and then use the computer with a choice of fonts to make their work look quite professional. Justa does that.

There were two fourth grade teachers. Someone whispered to Justa, "They are fairies." The only fairies that Justa knew about were imaginary, delicate, fluttering creatures. These two were interesting looking, big, and tall wearing long fascinating raccoon coats that were the rage of the time. It was many years later before she grasped what the girls were trying to tell her. It was apparent that she didn't know much about anything. That made learning so much fun for her. Justa developed into the instigator of many exciting adventures that she shared with Jim all those years.

She had a red headed male English teacher who gave spelling tests every day but didn't save the grades. Justa always got 100. So one day in his class she just had fun deliberately writing everything phonetically. The next day the teacher announced that a strange thing had happened the previous day. One of his best students had a problem with the test and was unable to get any words spelled correctly. He said that he hadn't been taking the grades but this day he did. He only counted three grades for that period and averaged in a zero for Justa. That kept her off of the honor roll that term. He really thought she'd complain or her parents would come in, and he'd probably have changed it. However, she said nothing but learned something. Not everyone appreciates her sense of humor.

A man learns to skate by staggering about making a fool of himself; indeed, he progresses in all things by making a fool of himself

—George Bernard Shaw

HER MOTHER, LAURA, SET A GOOD EXAMPLE

Laura was not only Justa's mother but also an excellent example of how valuable a homemaker was to her family and community. She not only organized her household, cooked, cleaned, did laundry, gardened, shopped, supplied transportation, took care of her husband's and children's needs. She also tended her mother and youngest sister when they needed her. She was the popular teacher of the young people's Sunday school class. She gave book reviews. She was active in Garden Club and the Ladies Aid Society. She and John would sometimes get all dressed up and go to the YM where they danced beautifully with the other dancers. When the depression hit, the executive position that John had was gone. He had worked for the National Watch Case Company in Elgin, Illinois. Now he was given a job traveling and selling, but there were no buyers. Fortunately they had lived more frugally than necessary and had saved enough to take care of their family and help others. They had planted fruit trees—apple, pear, and cherry. They had strawberry, raspberry, and blueberry bushes. They grew all kinds of vegetables and canned a great deal.

There were many needy people. The especially sad ones were the tramps. They would knock at the door and ask if they could have food or sometimes if there was work for food. Laura would invite them in just as any friend, give them bathroom privileges, a chance to wash up, feed them a nice meal, and give them something else if they appeared to need it and send them on their way. That would be dangerous today. Actually they did have one burglary which could have been related to this policy. When they arrived home from church one evening, they found that their home had been broken into. The antique lock box in which they kept their important papers was gone. They were saddened when they found it missing, but it was located behind the garage with their papers scattered about. Most important to Laura were the curls cut from John's head when he was a baby. They were still there in the little envelope where his mother had placed them. Apparently baby curls aren't a priority for someone stealing because he needs food and money. John's mother had saved them. Laura had also. Justa treasured them until she gave to Laurie her mother's locket with the curls.

Justa never really suffered from the depression. As for clothing, she could look in the window of any department store and pick out what she liked. However, she didn't buy it. She just showed Laura who nodded and said, "Oh, yes, we can do that. Bargain but attractive fabric was found. A beautiful dress was created and was certainly as nice and probably higher quality that the store offering. All this was an education for Justa. She had her own little sewing machine and made clothes for her dolls. The basement of their house had a room completely furnished with child size furniture. Justa used that until she finished grade school.

Justa's parents were hard workers and practical. When they were young, they bought property that included one whole block along a nice street. They personally built an attractive bungalow, lived there for awhile and then sold it when they built another. They had a grass tennis court on one side. When the children came, they still had one lot to sell and one on the corner big enough for all the neighborhood children to play baseball and other games. Around the corner from this playground was the home of Miss Gilillan, their grade school principal. Some children were afraid of her, but she was nice and never objected to any noise or activity. One day during a ball game Justa's brother hit a hooked ball that went across the property line and crashed into her basement window. She wasn't home, but he went to his parents to ask what he should do. He was told that as soon as she came home he would tell her what happened, say he was sorry and that he would pay for the repairs. He did as told and always had a good relationship with her. This middle class family was very active in the Methodist Church. Laura had five sisters, and they all showed up with their families on Sunday. She always fed them. This gave everyone an extended family. Laura was an exceptional woman who might have called herself a housewife, but I doubt that she would say "just a housewife". Everyone who knew her considered her special.

HER BASEMENT PLAYROOM A REAL HOME

Justa wanted to be like her mother. She loved her basement playroom. It was her private house where she could mimic Laura tending her dolls as her mother tended her. She had all the equipment to do that. She probably got her creativity from Laura. Justa was a very happy child. She seemed to enjoy everything and didn't know what one pretty little blonde playmate meant when she said she was bored. Justa didn't understand the word. She wished she could experience that. Luckily she never did.

When Justa and her brother were very young, the family would go to Crystal Lake, and they'd all go swimming. Initially there were no formal lessons. Their Dad just tossed them in the water, and they splashed around with the parents in the water nearby. Then they had lessons at the YW and YM and at summer camp until they became very proficient. They both loved their camp experiences and learned more about swimming, diving, nature, canoeing, sailing, archery, horseback riding and getting along with people. Justa was chosen "Indian Princess" her first summer at camp. That was the honor for the outstanding camper. It was like "Miss America" of the campground.

HE WORKED WITH HUMOR

Justa's Dad, John, worked for the National Watch Case Co. which was owned by two Jewish men, Sol and S.C. He was a good employee, and they were good employers. They respected each other, but at home at dinnertime John would tell funny stories imitating their accents. He was fond of them and not in any way mean about this. One day when Sol said, "That writing's terrible." John replied, "Well, you must realize, Sir, that all great men have poor penmanship." Sol looked up, scratched his head and replied, "You know, Yanny, come to think of it, I don't write so goot myself." Another story that John often told was about a clothing store when a customer asked for a specific color. The merchant turned to the clerk and said, "Turn on the blue light, Abie, the man vants a blue suit." He always kept them laughing. Often we wait for the speaker to end his story so that we might tell ours. When a family member talked too long or another wished to speak, John would say, "Do you know what a bore is? He's the guy who talks about his kid when you want to talk about yours." When asked how many hours he worked a day, he replied, "Well, I work 24 hours a day. Then I go back at night to finish."

NEW FRIENDS IN NEW NEIGHBORHOOD

Justa's family moved away to a bigger house. Both girls had been in Girl Scouts, but Justa became active in the Tri-Y where she served as president for several years, and the girls didn't see each other much any more. But Justa always appreciated what they had meant to her. She still has a postal card that her friend's father sent to her when she was little. It has a picture of a cat. When the card was squeezed, the cat meowed. Justa was terribly saddened when he had to be admitted to the Elgin State Hospital, a mental institution. He was always so good to Justa. People didn't realize then, and few do now, that this is possibly caused by a chemical imbalance of the brain. There should be more understanding and no stigma attached any more than with cancer or heart disease all of which they experienced in the extended family.

JUSTA WAS DELIGHTED WHEN GRANDMA AND AUNT EV CAME TO LIVE WITH THEM

Laura's father died at a very young age. There were no antibiotics for his serious infection. Her mother, Grandma Shales, was left with six girls. Laura was the one they turned to. This grandparent was the only one that Justa ever really knew well. She was such a sweet lady. After her girls were raised, she moved into John and Laura's house with her youngest daughter, Evelyn. Justa loved having them there and has happy memories of the time. During a really big storm one night Justa went to the upstairs landing window overlooking the back garden. Standing there looking out was her Grandma. Some old ladies would be afraid and shaking with fright, but she did a wonderful thing. She put her arm around Justa's shoulders and said, "Isn't it beautiful?" Justa grew up seeing the beauty of storms. When Justa developed a hammer toe that was troubling her, her grandmother heated some oil and massaged the foot. She offered to do it whenever Justa wanted the treatment. She was so appreciative of being able to live with them that she wanted to help in any way that she could.

This grandmother was a brave woman, but she was skeptical of new technology. She was hesitant to use the telephone and always asked Justa to take on that tough job for her. Laura's older sister was likewise doubtful of new equipment. She never would use a noisy electric vacuum cleaner. She stuck with her quiet Bissell sweeper. Her Aunt Ev had a good job and nice clothes, the same size that Justa wore. They were both small. When Justa started dating, her aunt loaned her some lovely clothes, even a beautiful fur jacket. Justa was happy many years later when she could reciprocate.

PRIVATE PLAYGROUND AT HOME

Now back to her childhood. At the bigger house in the new neighborhood, John had built playground equipment; so they could high jump, pole vault, and do exercises on the horizontal bar. One time Justa was swinging by her knees and fell and hurt both wrists. There was concern that there could be permanent damage. She's very thankful that that never developed. They served her for a long life of tending her family and of use playing the piano, and organ, writing, sewing, tennis playing, golf, computing, and gardening. Laura was in the garden club and had a beautiful flower garden and they had nice shrubs bordering the whole back yard. This is where John decided one day to trim the hedge. When Justa came home from school and said, "Daddy, what have you done?" He replied, "Please don't pick on me too. Your mother is unhappy, the neighbors don't like it, and the fire department came." Well, in a few weeks people were admiring how wonderful everything looked. It was just what the hedge needed. Justa remembered that occasion years later when she was grounds chair for the condominium and there was such a fuss about trimming hedges. She was for it, because she knew that plants grow back.

QUARANTINED FOR MUMPS NEIGHBOR FOR POLIO

One summer Justa's older brother, Wes, developed mumps. They were both quarantined for two weeks. Then her brother was able to go out to play and attend all activities. Justa did not get the mumps; so she was quarantined for another two weeks. She didn't think that that was fair. She said, "That is inequitable." That was a pretty big word for a youngster. She was a creative child. On the property adjourning the back of her yard there lived two children. The older girl developed polio; so her younger sister was also stuck at home. The two young girls made friends without ever leaving their property, and they didn't touch each other. They made a new friendship and played all kinds of games; so neither one became lonely. They just communicated through the opening in the hedge.

HIGH SCHOOL LESSONS LEARNED BEYOND SUBJECT

1932-1936

In 1932 on her first day at high school Justa learned a lesson on prejudice. In study hall students were assigned seats alphabetically. The teacher called her forward. She said, Miss Spalding, would you like to have your seat changed? Justa didn't have a clue as to what she meant. Charles Smith was in the seat behind her, and he was black. What difference did that make? To Justa people are people regardless of their color, sex, religion, or position. She is as comfortable with the chairman of the board as the pest control man. She learned more of prejudice when she taught at Scott Field during WW2. Some Texan GI's insisted they'd go AWOL before they'd be in a class with a "Nigger" instructor. She asked them if they needed a brain surgeon and the only available was black, would they go without the surgery? They were angry with her for that stand. Of course, she does not approve of groups that teach hate and killing.

Justa's parents were hard workers and practical. When they were young, they bought property that included one whole block along a nice street. They personally built an attractive bungalow, lived there for awhile and then sold it when they built another. They had a grass tennis court on one side. When the children came, they still had one lot to sell and one on the corner big enough for all the neighborhood children to play baseball and other games.

THEIR CLIQUE

The only way to have a friend is to be one.

—Ralph Waldo Emerson

In high school Justa had eight close, nice girl friends that were apparently a "clique". They thoroughly enjoyed each other and didn't realize how some jealous girls viewed them. Her closest friend during high school was Mary Lou. John drove the girls to high school. Justa had to be ready on time. She was although sometimes that meant skipping breakfast. When they picked up Mary, sometimes they would have to wait, and then Justa could smell food on Mary's breath. That was the only time that she got upset with her friend, waiting for her to eat when she had skipped breakfast to be one time. However, she never complained. One day Mary got an unkind note that startled the group. "You damned conceited little devils." Justa didn't understand this because she was always friendly with everyone. She was always full of energy and popular with the boys. She dated a lot, even went to the senior prom as a fresh freshman; so she ended up going to five senior proms. Nowadays that might mean a lot of sex. However, because of her training, she was able to attend great events and get to know many good people and remain a virgin until her wedding night.

SOME FOOLISH THINGS IN HER LIFE

Justa was a good teenager but normal in that she did some foolish things. After a dance several times, she went with a group to drive to the South Elgin stone quarry where they could swim. She wore a swimsuit that was "smocked" with elastic thread. One night she went off the high dive, and when she hit the water, the suit went down beneath her breasts and had to be quickly pulled up. It was sufficiently dark that probably no one actually saw it, but she was so modest that she was very embarrassed. Later she realized that wasn't the major problem. It really wasn't a very safe idea to be swimming down there in the dark and without lifeguards. And perhaps even more foolish, she did this. She was all dressed up and at a party when someone suggested going tobogganing. She loved life. She never wanted to miss anything. Of course, she would go. Friends offered to take her home to change to appropriate clothes, but she didn't want for them to be inconvenienced and insisted that's she'd be all right. She was in a dress and wearing silk stockings, and of course she about froze to death. The skin on her legs has never been the same. Sometimes we have to learn the hard way. Of course, there were many more, but who can remember all that? She was lucky to have such wonderful friends and good schools in Elgin, Illinois then.

STILL KIDS AND FUN AT HOME

They didn't have to go out and spend a lot of money to have fun. At Justa's house, she would play the piano, and friends would sing. Often they would roll up the big oriental carpet, put records on the Victrola and dance. They played charades or sometimes spin the milk bottle. In the back yard they could play on the sports equipment that John had built. Laura's beautiful garden was seldom disturbed. Justa's brother was allowed to have all kinds of motorcycles and old cars in the garage and on the driveway. He had great pleasure working on them. His mother looked out one day and saw him going by the house standing on his head on a motor cycle. She was a great lady who let her children grow up, and she was proud of them. With his own sons her brother didn't allow them to have motorcycles. Justa did, but she dreaded that sound when she could hear it when she was playing golf and knew that it meant her son, Wes, was looking for her and needed something. One day as he was riding his cycle in a line of cars on a busy street, a woman drove out of a store exit and ran right into him, throwing his body in the air, dropping him on top of her car. That could have been disastrous, but he survived and continued to ride. Justa was not the dare devil that her brother was, but she stood on her head on the diving board, even the high board. She also stood on the shoulders of a young man who was on the aquaplane. She was adventurous but in different ways than her brother. As an adult he was a very responsible successful, electrical engineer, but even as a senior citizen he competed in triathlons and ski races, and he climbed to the top of Kilimanjaro.

RESPOND QUICKLY TO CHAIR CHAIR

Justa helped at summer Bible School. She was playing the piano and leading the little children singing, "Can a little child like me thank the father fittingly?" A youngster tugged on her skirt crying "Chair, chair." Justa replied, "Now please sit down. You have a chair." "Can a little child like me thank the father fittingly?" "Chair Chair." "Please sit down." "Can a little child like me?" Then the lights came on in Justa's brain, and she realized the little tot was holding her crotch and in great need. She assisted and treated the youngster with love and kindness. The singing continued in a few minutes. And Justa had learned a lesson, just one of the billion or so she still had to learn.

THE LESSON SHE NEVER LEARNED

About the worst offense Justa committed in grade school was talking too much to her friend, Carna. They had to stay after school and write 10 times "I must not talk. I must not talk." She had exceptionally fine teachers, but that particular lesson she never learned. You may have noticed that she always has something to say. For example as a young lady meeting at the church parsonage to organize a youth fellowship, the pastor stopped and asked the group, "Would you like to hear what you said and how you sounded?" This was before the days of all the electronic equipment; so they were startled when they learned that he had hidden a microphone behind a picture on the piano. He played it back. Justa heard her voice all the way through saying, "I have an idea." Then she'd give her idea, and they would tell her that it was great and ask her if she'd take care of the project, and she'd answer "Oh, yes, gladly". To this day her daughter lectures her but with affection, "Mom, you're supposed to be an intelligent woman. There's a simple word spelled, "N O". You really should learn it."

DANCING FOREVER

Justa in one of many costumes her mother made for her.

Justa took dancing lessons from the time she was a little child. Her mother made many very fine costumes for her. When justa and Jim moved to Freedom Village, an antique dealer was thrilled to buy the one costume that her mother had saved all those years and a framed picture of Justa wearing the beautiful dress. When Justa and her brother were of an age to take ballroom dancing, they were most fortunate to have a French lady, Mademoiselle Yingst as their teacher. The girls were dressed in lovely clothing. The boys had to wear shirts and ties, coats, patent leather shoes and white gloves. As the young people entered the ballroom, the boys bowed, and the girls curtsied first to Mademoiselle Yingst and then to each other. Then the boy offered his arm to the girl and led her to a chair where he bowed to her as she was seated. When he wanted a girl to dance, he walked to her chair, bowed and asked, "May I have the honor of the following dance?" She would rise and curtsy as she accepted with, "I would be delighted." Her parents enjoyed dancing too.

Fortunately years later Justa found a wonderful young man who was also a good dancer. They still dance at every opportunity. At black tie affairs, he wears his black patent leather shoes. He did that with their dinner dance club on their 65th wedding anniversary party at the Bird Key Yacht Club in Sarasota. I would call them octogenarians, but I just realized that he isn't one any more. At church recently when the leader asked for people to share their "joys and concerns", Justa took a turn and said, "My joy is being here with my 90-year-old husband." There were smiles about the room. Then she hesitated and actually looked sad as she said, "Tomorrow that will no longer be true." The congregation shared her apparent sadness not knowing what was happening whether he was running away with some blonde, she was running, or one of them was dying. But when she said, "I'll be living with a 91-year-old man." Hesitation and then she added, "with the same name". The leader then very nicely asked about other birthdays and anniversaries that week and everyone sang happy something to the group. When the service was over, one of the ladies that Justa had just met recently said something that Justa wants to remember and suggests we could all do the same.

In response to *"How are you?"* she replied, *"Bursting with the joy of living."* That was followed with a most beautiful smile. What a fine example for all to follow! Justa heard recently that this lovely, elderly lady is getting married again.

REMEMBERING

Recollection is the only paradise from which we cannot be turned out.

— Jean Paul Richter

Justa and Jim flew back to Illinois to attend a wonderful party given by one her classmates who had been out of the country since college days. One man came up and called her by name, and she immediately recognized him although they had not seen each other since grade school. He reminded her that they had the same birthdays and that he had attended her 12th birthday party. There had been music for dancing, of course! She had taught him to dance. She didn't remember that, but she should have. At home the family had loved to stand around the piano and sing as Laura played. Justa soon replaced her mother at the bench. She played the viola in the grade school and high school orchestra. Her big brother played the clarinet and was able to be in the band and wear a fancy uniform. I think she was a little jealous when everyone said how handsome he was. There were no uniforms in the orchestra. Although through the years she tried ukulele, guitar, drums, accordion, and trombone. Jim was always patient. It was only when she got carried away with her drums that he very nicely said, "Would you mind practicing in the garage?" And so she did. As an octogenarian she's settled on piano and electronic

Brother Wes in band uniform

organ. When she is waiting for someone or something, she just plays a few tunes. Both bring her great pleasure.

NOT MAY QUEEN BUT THE MOST CREDITS

When it was almost time to choose the May Queen in high school, Justa knew that one of her little group would be chosen, and the others would be attendants. She was startled when the announcement was made that there would be no May Queen that year. She never questioned why. Perhaps some wise adult knew something she didn't know, and there would be jealousy and a problem. That was unexpected, but she was also surprised on graduation night to hear the announcement that she had more credits than anyone in the school's history. She figured that it wasn't as impressive as it sounded. She loved school and took every subject they would let her take. So that, along with the grades, gave her a lot of credits.

THE ELECTRIC APPLIANCE BUSINESS PLUGGED IN AND TURNED ON? LAURA HELPED AND JUSTA TOO

The world is filled with willing people; some willing to work, the rest willing to let them.

—Robert Frost

When Justa started high school, her father, John had joined with another ex-executive to start a small electric appliance business. When John realized that his partner was so accustomed to sitting behind a big desk and giving orders to his secretary and that he would add nothing to the business, John and Laura bought his share. That was the turning point. Laura, the organizer, came aboard. John was the super salesman. From that point on, the store was on its way to becoming a huge success. At first they had rented a store building but couldn't afford to completely stock it. They would drive to Chicago regularly and buy one of a kind of the bigger items. When it sold, it would be reordered. Before they could afford a truck, Justa was embarrassed when the family car had the front right seat removed so that a washing machine could be carried in there and delivered. Purchasers would often call during dinnertime to say that something didn't work. John patiently and courteously questioned the caller to ask if the device was plugged in and turned on. Invariably that was the only problem because they didn't let anything leave the store that wasn't in proper condition. He was a good-looking man with a big smile. He was honest, hard working, well liked.

Justa was amused watching her parents in action. When a lady would enter the front door of the store, John would look at Laura for help. He was handsome, and all the ladies thought that they were special. John would put on that beautiful smile, look at the lady coming in and say, "Dottie, how is my favorite girl?" or some such thing. She didn't know that Laura had softly whispered her name to John so he would know who she was. Her parents were both very personable and made many friends. They soon were able to hire a number of employees and be relieved from doing so much work themselves. They built their own building. The store was a big success.

When they decided to sell "mangles" to iron big items such as sheets and tablecloths, they took Justa to the factory to be trained in their use. As a high school student, she sat in the store window and demonstrated how to do this properly. She also gave home demonstrations. She only made one serious mistake. A lady, who fortunately was a friend of her parents, asked if it was all right to use the mangle to iron a dress right over the buttons. Justa replied, "Oh, yes." She remembered being taught that. However, she didn't know about this new material they were using for buttons that melted when heated. If I have the story correct, the buttons became a permanent part of the dress. She only worked at the store part time because she was active in clubs at the school—French club, math club, played viola in orchestra, played piano for vocal groups, and was president of Tri-Y Club for a couple years. Every Friday Justa went to the nearby beauty shop and for 50 cents (no tip) she had her long hair shampooed, put in rollers, dried, and arranged. It also cost 50 cents for most dry cleaning. The wonderful sandwiches at the Star Hamburger Shop went up from 5 cents to 10 cents, and were they good! In 2006 when she and Jim stopped in for a hot dog at a state park, they were handed a bill for $11.61. Justa said, "Over $11 for two hot dogs with nothing on them?" The clerk said, "Well, the water is $2.50 each." Justa replied, "Thank you, but I'm not thirsty." Of course, she was after hiking the trails, but not that thirsty. She was a depression baby.

THE REPAIR LADY IN FATIGUES

She did help at the store again briefly at the end of World War 2 when they needed someone to manage the repair shop. There were just no other available qualified individuals around. She donned a fatigue suit and repaired radios. Customers were surprised to see a young lady there able to do the job. Actually it was easy for her because she had taught this for three years. What they didn't understand was that if the radio was completely dead, it was very easy to solve the problem. It was more difficult when there was an intermittent problem with a device that would work and then would not work. The most annoying one was a small Zenith radio. It looked easy, but when she took the cover off, roaches ran every place! She yelled.

She said that she would have been less startled by a grizzly bear! Men came running in. One man was from the dry cleaning establishment, and tossed some chemical on the creatures. One of the men used a soldering iron in the attack. Another zapped some with electricity. Once she recovered from the shock, she looked at the job before her. To her it appeared that someone had thrown in coils, condensers, resisters, wires, and vacuum tubes, and covered it all with solder. It was so small and unclean that it was difficult to see any circuits. She calmed down, brushed off some dirt and could see what she needed to do. She could fix it but thought it wasn't worth the effort, but that wasn't her decision to make. She did her job and then went on to a more worthwhile project. A friend stopped in to see her and not realizing the dangers of the workbench, tossed a beautiful new coat on top of a hot soldering iron. She was not accustomed to her friend in such surroundings. The coat was badly damaged by the time that Justa smelled it and turned around and saw what had happened. The friend didn't understand the many different roles that Justa had played since they were children together.

HOW ONE CIGARETTE CHANGED HER LIFE ALTHOUGH SHE DIDN'T SMOKE IT —1937

Justa's next door neighbor, Bill, invited her to go to dinner and dance in Chicago. His friend, Bud, had a date, and they'd be a foursome. Then Bud called that Joe, his cousin from California, would be in town and wanted to join them. They weren't crazy about the idea but agreed, although that meant that four sat in the back seat. Bill's parents were out of town. They owned the Cadillac-Oldsmobile agency. His mother had said that he could drive her new car but there could be no smoking. He promised. Everything went fine, and they were having a good time.

On route 20 driving back from Chicago to Elgin Joe lit up a cigarette. Bill cried out, "NO, NO, NO." He had promised. He turned just enough to take the cigarette away. As he did the front right wheel went off the edge onto the loose gravel. He was driving at the highway speed of the day, but it was fast enough that he lost control of the car. It rolled over five times and knocked over a telephone pole and cut WGN off the air. Bill was thrown across the highway. Justa was the only one walking around when drivers stopped to help. She said that she had crawled out through the smashed windshield. They didn't think that was possible. But she was small, and she did. Strangers were bringing her hats and purses and anything they had found. If I have the story correct, the four in the backseat had to be cut out. Ambulances took all six to Sherman Hospital in Elgin. Although she had blood on her, Justa insisted that she was all right.

The only one who walked away

As soon as she thought that the other five were taken care of, she asked a deputy to take her home. She insisted that she was fine. She thought so at first. She slipped into bed and didn't report to her parents until breakfast. She couldn't eat for a couple days, but then when she got some food inside of her, she had a severe abdominal pain and had to admit that she was hurt. When her parents called their doctor friend, he came right over and said "appendicitis". In retrospect she is convinced that it was not the correct diagnosis. That he was wrong. After all that rolling around her intestines were knotted up. The surgeon also admitted inadvertently cutting her ovaries when he did an appendectomy. That's hard to understand. Justa paid little attention to all the talk. She only wanted out and back to living. Years later when she and Jim were unable to have their own biological babies, the doctor blamed it on his service in WW 2 in the S. Pacific. It could have been either, neither, or both. The accident certainly didn't help. The boys who caused the problem sued the driver for negligence.

STUNG ON CANOE TRIP ADVENTURE

Who dares nothing, need hope for nothing.

—Johann von Schiller

Justa and friend, Mary Dane Cory, were in charge of a wilderness canoe trip for campers from Camp Indianoqua in Madison, Wisconsin, 1938. It was quite an adventure and great fun for the youngsters. They prepared their meals along the way and slept on the ground at night. Then they reached an area where the water was so shallow that they could not continue. That's when they learned what "portage" meant. They got out of their canoes and waded ashore pulling and then lifting their canoes. They had to turn their canoes upside down and with one at the bow and one at the stern, they would carry them along the shore until they found deeper water. But before they started they had to repack their supplies that had to last several days. It was not a smooth path, but they were young and managed the rough ground all right.

They sang and made it a joyous occasion as they watched for possible deeper water. Justa was at the end of the line to be certain that her charges were all right. Then she heard a scream and saw a red canoe go up and seem to fly through the air. And then other canoes and screams. Mary Dane and Justa put down their canoes and ran from both ends of the line to determine the cause. There were bees buzzing all over the area.

One of the girls had stepped into a hive. All the campers who were close to her were stung. It's so long ago that Justa can't remember how they quickly got the girls away from the bees or how they treated the stings. What she does remember vividly is what happened to those who were closest to the hive. Their stings caused severe swelling in some cases around the eyes, and in others between the fingers so that their hands looked webbed. At that time they weren't aware of the fact that they could be allergic and possibly die from the attacks. They comforted the victims the best they could, checked on the water depth and decided to try to get back out there.

They lugged the canoes off the dangerous land and packed their supplies in the bows to have the weight balanced a little better. They put those stung the worst lying flat in the bottoms and the stronger at the stern. Some couldn't possibly hold a paddle. Justa reminded each girl who was in charge of her canoe how she had to paddle to go in the right direction because she had no help from up front. They were given a quick snack for the energy they would need. No one knew it but Justa had severe menstrual cramps. Her period was just starting, and she hurt. But off they went with Justa leading the singing and guiding the boats that didn't seem to want to go the proper direction.

When Justa was offered this councilor job, she was told that the youngsters were "rich kids from the north shore of Chicago". They had to have the best. It would appear that they had had enough excitement for one day, but no, these kids must have really needed adventure, because the powers that be presented more. A clash of thunder and then lightening and rain! They should not be on the water, but now they weren't that close to shore, and it looked uninhabitable anyway. She was responsible for them. What should they do? She saw tall stalks of something in the water closer to shore.

But worst of all—there was some male character in those high fishing boots fastened to his rubber pants, or whatever you call them. He was waving at them and trying to get them to paddle toward him. Some pervert? Oh, no. She couldn't handle that. Oh, yes. Thank God. This was one time that she was glad to accept help. It was Mr. Metcalf, the camp director, trying to get them to come to shore. These weren't spoiled kids at all. They were sharp, and they paddled hard to move to safety. There were helpers awaiting them as they got their canoes close enough, and then they waded or were lifted through that water with the tall grass and goodness knows what else was in there. No one even mentioned possible snakes and other creatures. Several qualified drivers were ready with trucks to handle campers and canoes as the storm rolled on. They were successful in getting every one and all the equipment loaded and headed for home. Although they were dirty and wet, before long they were all back at camp, had had hot showers, and were cleaned up. The nurse tended the sickest ones, but even they were bragging to the younger kids about their adventures. And the ones who missed this trip were begging, *"Miss Phyl, can we go the next time? Please, Miss Phyl? Please?"*

ACCIDENT DELAYED MARRIAGE

Justa and Jim were planning a big formal wedding in 1940 after her graduation from college. He was driving on route 20 from Elgin to Chicago where he was employed. Suddenly he saw a bad truck accident on his right, but as he slowed down and looked up so did the truck driver in front of him, but HE stopped. Jim couldn't, but he turned his wheels trying to avoid a collision, but it was too late. His car went under the back end of that huge truck. Jim was severely injured. His head, jaw, nose, sinuses, and chest would never be the same. Every part of his body was injured. An ambulance took him to Elmhurst hospital. Justa and his Dad drove there as soon as they were alerted.

Justa was distraught. As soon as she saw him, she fussed at the doctors and nurses, "If it's broken, operate, fix it!" They tried to explain that he was in shock, and that this couldn't be done immediately. His mouth was full of blood. She said, ""Please clean it out. He'll choke on it. He can't breath." His Dad got on the phone immediately and called an Elgin doctor friend and made arrangements to move him there where both families were well known, and they knew the doctors. They rode in the ambulance with him and tried to comfort him, but they needed consoling too.

The healing took a long time. She would stay at the hospital with him for hours. One day he said, "You might as well go home. You can't do anything here." It hurt her, but she left. When she got home the phone was ringing, and he was asking her to please return. She did immediately. The jaw was wired shut for what seemed an eternity. A dear aunt used a blender and prepared every nourishing food she could for him to take through straws. The wired jaw just wouldn't heal; so then it was put in a silver cast. When they were finally married at a big beautiful formal wedding, his jaw was still in a silver cast. The injuries caused him lifetime problems.

Little minds are tamed and subdued by misfortune; but great minds rise above them

.—Washington Irving

A CHILD IS MISSING

Justa asks, *"Do I have permission to check the pool?"*

It was the summer of 1937. Justa was hired to be a councilor at the Beloit (Wisconsin) Camp Rotary. She had been swimming all her life, had not only passed junior and senior life saving tests, but also was certified by the Red Cross to pass others on these tests. The first day she was assigned a group and a list of campers to be in her cabin and her responsibility. She had checked in the girls and was helping them to unpack and organize their cots. Someone came to her door and said, "Are all your girls here?" "Yes." "Are there any extra girls here?" "No. Is there a problem?" "Yes, one child is missing." "Has anyone searched along the woods, the river? "Yes, Yes." "What the about the pool?" "No."

"Do I have permission to do that?" "Yes." "Who will take care of my girls?" "I will."

Justa ran down the hill and through the woods to the pool. It wasn't like the modern pools. The sides sloped and were slimy and slippery. The water wasn't clear. Justa slid in immediately. She surface dived and swam from end to end, knowing she wouldn't find anything, hoping she would, and hoping she wouldn't. She couldn't see anything in this water. Then as she thought she had covered the whole pool completely, she reached out her right arm, and her hand touched something. Oh, it couldn't be, but it was. It was a child's foot. She had taught life saving and gone over this so many times. There she was with the proper grip and getting the child out of the water and onto her stomach with head to side after clearing the mouth, doing what was then called "Artificial Respiration". Now CPR is used. At one stage she had taught, "Out goes the bad air, in comes the good." At another time she taught, "Hands on, swing forward, release, relax." At this point she was saying, "Hands on, swing forward, release, relax." As she worked she also called out instructions to those around to call the nurse and the doctor and the emergency service and the director and get blankets and get any other children out of the area. She had moments when she thought she was making progress. Then, "Thanks, Patty, slide the blanket over the child without losing my rhythm. Say this with me, "Hands on, swing forward, release, relax." I almost feel some warmth. When you have it, slide over and relieve me. No questions now please. Marie, keep those people away. Hands on, swing forward, release, relax. Thanks, Patty. Just stay with it. Who are you? Right this way, Doctor. You're not the doctor? You're from the fire department? You can't use that Pulmotor on this little child. That will just ruin her insides. That's too much oxygen for a little child."

"Oh, hello, you must be the doctor. You're the photographer? Yes, I found her. No, we don't know. Oh, please go away now. How could the newspaper get someone here before the doctor could arrive? We don't want to lose the rhythm. We're fighting for the child's life. Oh, Julie, do you think we are getting anywhere? Oh, hello. You are the doctor? Thank goodness. Yes, we'll step back. What's he doing, Julie? Oh, take my hand; pray, Julie, pray. What's he doing? He's covering her up. Oh, Julie!"

This was devastating for Justa. She felt so terrible because she could not save the little girl although she was assured over and over again that the child was actually dead at the time that Justa found her. It was just that they all wanted so much for the child to survive. Apparently she had been told that when she went to camp, she would be able to swim. She must have found the pool, walked in and on the slippery surface slid right down. She couldn't walk on that surface, and she couldn't swim. This was just speculation, but some thought that it all happened before the camp program had even started. Justa had to talk to everybody including the campers, councilors, parents and the reporters because she found the child.

The woman who was to be in charge of the swimming and waterfront was so distraught that she was unable to perform that function. Justa was asked to take charge. She set up a program that didn't allow anyone in the pool except at fixed times. There was a board there with an identifying pin for each camper. When one entered the pool, she took off her pin and fastened it to her suit. She replaced the pin to the board when she got out. Each swimmer had a buddy with whom to swim. There was a lifeguard for every five swimmers. The program worked fine, but of course it was too late for the one little girl who couldn't wait. For a long time she couldn't get over the terrible feeling that she couldn't save this child. It was worse when people treated her as a heroine because she found the body. She was assured that she couldn't do anything more than she did do, but it still hurts.

Into each life some rain must fall.

—Henry Wadsworth Longfellow

COLLEGE LESSONS LEARNED FROM PROFESSORS IN ADDITION TO SUBJECT MATTER

Justa heard the story of "prove this chair is not here". The answer was "What chair?" This story reminded Justa of her freshman course at Rockford College when a professor taught her a good lesson. She was a math major taking her first philosophy course. In her immature state, she said to the professor, "I don't think I will like philosophy. There are no definite answers. I'm majoring in math because when one says, '2 + 2 = 4,' there's no question about it." The professor responded, "Miss Spalding, any time you would like to write a paper proving to me that 2 + 2 = 4, I'll be glad to read and evaluate it." She took the challenge and spent the night writing a paper trying to prove this.

She ended up learning a great deal from this man. They got along very well and had many good debates. Early in the game he was trying to teach her the philosophy of the man who said, "Things are not real. They are just thoughts in your head." So Justa said to him, "Then if that's true, why don't you put all those books in your head instead of carrying that heavy load in the green bag every day?" I don't know how he put up with her, but he seemed to enjoy her ridiculous thoughts and helped to educate her.

Her religion professor asked for a paper on the four gospels, Matthew, Mark, Luke, and John. Justa thought, "We've been through this. How dumb!" She did study and did write the paper, but she chose to write the whole thing in rhyme. The professor was the minister at the Temple in Chicago. He was wise, read through her paper, and grinned as he did. Then he sat down and wrote a response completely in rhyme. This occurred 70 years ago, but she still remembers his final words. He told her that it was accurate and clever but that in the future they had better stick to "prose prosaic".

Rockford College was a wonderful school where classes were so small and professors actually knew the students, and students could learn so much from them beyond the actual subject. Her math professor was brilliant but often wrote on the blackboard "x squared" when she said, "y cubed". She was loved and gently corrected by a student. One day when she came to class and she was told, "Miss McGavock, you are wearing a black shoe on your left foot and a brown on the right." She smiled and answered, "That's funny, I have a pair just like this at home." She is also reputed to have planned a lovely dinner party. Everything was perfection until she realized that the reason that no one arrived was that she had forgotten to mail the invitations. In spite of these stories she was an excellent teacher. One lesson learned was that even geniuses do make mistakes. It was in these math classes that Justa met Ellen when they were the only two students. She liked and respected her immediately, and they have kept in touch through the years. Ellen married a mathematician, and together they wrote a couple math books.

JIM OR MAYO NOT JIM AND MAYO

He who chooses the beginning of a road chooses the place it leads to. It is the means that determine the end.

—Harry Emerson Fosdick

Dr. Johnson, her physics professor, was another bright, pleasant individual and very helpful. She is the one who offered Justa the opportunity for a job with Mayo Clinic when they asked the good doctor for her recommendation. That was before Justa's graduation, and she had to decide whether to take the job or marry Jim. There was no thought of doing both. It was one or the other. In those days if a good man asked a lady to marry him and said that he loved her and wanted to care for her all her life, she would be foolish not to accept. They appeared to be a perfect fit. She had dated enough to realize how special he was. It seems she made the right choice. The lesson here is that there is more to teaching than covering the subject. It's understanding the pupils and helping them in decision making that can influence the rest of their lives. Justa does, however, advise all females to develop their own skills before they marry so that they don't ever have to feel financially dependent on another individual and be called just a housewife. Justa had the opportunity to improve her skills by her work during World War 2.

A SEABEE AND A WIRE SERVED THEIR COUNTRY

Their lives changed drastically when the Japanese bombed Pearl Harbor on December 7, 1941. Friends were drafted into service or volunteered, but Jim still had his jaw in a cast made of silver, and he had a 4F classification. Because of his accident the service didn't want him. Then July 17, 1942 the card came, "Uncle Sam needs you." Justa had been prepared to be "just a homemaker", but she actually had another job before that. Some of her skills plus her sense of humor were pluses. When they were perusing Uncle Sam's message, Justa was also reading the Chicago Tribune headline, "CQ, CQ, GIRLS; ARMY NEEDS YOU TO TEACH RADIO". The article stated, "For the first time the men who handle the delicate radio instruments on the big "flying fortresses may get their technical training from women instructors." Justa said to Jim, "I have those qualifications because of all the math and physics credits. Maybe I should apply." He agreed that she should. She did and was asked report ASAP to Scott Field near Belleville, Illinois. You've heard of WACS and WAVES and ROSIE THE RIVETER, but probably not the WIRES. Justa was soon to become one of the few WIRES, women in radio electronics. She went on to teach the men how to build and repair their transmitters and receivers.

Before she could do that they had to decide about Jim. He had a fraternity brother, Larry Buckmaster from Northwestern University. He was a naval officer and convinced Jim to join the navy. Larry was sure that there would be no question that Jim would be an officer with his excellent academic and employment record. They drove to Covington, Indiana for his enlistment. Jim was colorblind, and that kept him from officer's training. There were many decisions to be made. All this would change their lives significantly. Jim became a member of the 72nd Naval Construction Battalion, the famous Seabees, those wonderful men who often went in before the Marines to build the roads and housing. His division was credited with freeing Guam.

The pin and patch on her uniform read AAFTTC. That stands for Army Air Force Technical Training Command. The War Department hired her. Civil Service paid her. A letter from the AAF was in a small envelope the size of a little party invitation. It was khaki color. In the top left corner were the words WAR & NAVY DEPARTMENTS. They drove from Evanston to Belleville, Illinois arriving after dark. Suddenly Justa wondered what she had got into. Suddenly all she could see were GI's in fatigue suits on the streets or going into bars. They found the Traveler's Aid office to ask where they might sleep. "There's no room at the inn" was the answer and a story they were going to hear more than once. Then the woman looked at Justa and said, "Just a minute." She made a call to a friend who agreed that their daughter could move into the parents' room, and the daughter's room could be rented to Justa. Jim stayed with Justa that night, and in the morning she drove him to St. Louis, Missouri to the train station so he could get back to work. She drove back to Belleville and to Scott Field. She identified herself to get on base and received instructions on where to go next. As she walked along beside the men's dorms, the GIs whistled and called out, "HELLO, sweater girl!"

QUITE A TRANSITION FOR BOTH

Justa started in August, but Jim didn't have to report until December. He was still examining banks for the FDIC when she had their only car. He eventually had to close down the apartment alone and get everything into storage. He never complained. She was immediately given "classified" textbooks that would review electricity, transmitter, and receiver circuits that would be used. The new instructors were given crash courses on the specific equipment that they would teach. She also had to review Morse code, but she never had to teach that because she was needed on the science part. When she got back to Belleville that first night, her "landlady" asked if she would share her room with this other woman who would also be an instructor. She was glad to help out and found herself sharing a bed with a stranger and was completely innocent of the fact that this could be a problem. It wasn't.

Each day driving to the base Justa filled her car with GI's or anyone hitch-hiking along the roadside. There was a black woman who was intelligent, very nice, and hired to teach Morse code. Justa gave her transportation. Some Texas men couldn't understand how she could do that! She didn't know she couldn't! When the school was just starting and before the men were accustomed to having a female instructor, one young student tried to be funny. He asked for help. His transmitter was lying unplugged upside down on the bench. As Justa started to test it with her ohmmeter, he inserted the plug into the electric outlet. Of course, she got a nasty shock. It happened a couple times, but she quickly gained the men's respect. Most of them were very appreciative of her knowledge and teaching ability.

Who dares to teach must never cease to learn.

—John Cotton Dana

She taught an assortment of students. Some were quite young men. Others were successful businessmen and really put in the wrong place in the service. She felt sorry for some of them. When they wanted to go to the men's room, they had to come to her for a latrine pass. Some were very protective of her. One day at break time one of the young men offered her a cigarette. Two others came running up and said, "You didn't take a smoke from him, did you?" She didn't. She didn't smoke. If he was offering her something bad, she could have had a problem. She had no knowledge of drugs.

There was one young man who didn't keep quite as clean as the others thought he should in the presence of a lady. Apparently at night instead of bathing as he should, he kept a jar of cream by his bed and smeared that on his body. One night some of the men put some shoe polish in the cream. The next morning his body was covered with black "ointment". He had many volunteers who insisted that they were friends who wanted to help him with wire brushes to get cleaned up for inspection. He showed up for class that day with pink baby-like skin. Then he found it much easier to shower as the others did.

A St. Louis newspaper sent out a reporter to interview the females who had taken on this work. An article appeared when this was just beginning and before the women really knew what they were doing. He was impressed and called them "Women in Radio Electronics". That was the first that she actually knew she was a WIRE. She is not sure if the AAF gave them that name or the reporter, There were more articles written about the WIRES, but they are certainly not well known. They had some publicity during the war, and at one time Justa was asked if she wanted a commission. She was too busy to even think about that. At the end of the war, they were asked if they wanted to stay with Civil Service which would have given her some income up to this day. The war was over. They could go back to their lives. She asked for nothing. As far as Justa knows the WIRES have not had any of the perks of other service personnel.

She's a WIRE - WW2

HER NEXT CLASSROOM THE BALLROOM IN THE STEVENS HOTEL CHICAGO

After this school was established, they needed more training schools and took over the Stevens (later the Hilton) and Congress Hotels on Michigan Avenue in Chicago. The hotel ballrooms had partitions set up to make small classrooms. Justa was given the choice of going to Boca Raton, Florida or Chicago. She chose Chicago because her parents lived in Elgin, and she missed family. She often lectured on the late night shift. If she finished early enough, she literally ran across from Michigan Avenue to Wells St. to catch the train at the Chicago, Aurora, and Elgin station. There was a wonderful conductor there who would say, "Here she is. We can go now." When the train arrived in Elgin by the Elgin Watch Company parking lot, it was pitch black. Her car was the only one in the lot. She ran to her car and drove to her parent's home. It was late, and they were asleep. She had a little rest, breakfast with her parents and then took the train back to Chicago.

When Jim heard by slow mail what she was doing, he was worried about it. He thought that it just wasn't safe in that area late at night. As usual she probably was still too naïve to realize the dangers, but anyway she was too busy to spend time worrying. When the timing was such that she couldn't make the train, she would take a little room, the size of a small closet at the YMCA Hotel on Wabash Avenue. That was just around the corner from the hotels where she taught. Here she also had protection. One night as she took the elevator up to the room, and a man tried to get off after her. The elevator operator wouldn't let him off even though Justa wasn't aware of the man. Often her innocence could have caused her a problem, but perhaps it was what saved her.

DAILY LETTERS

The way to love anything is to realize it may be lost.
—G. K. Chesterton

Through all of this Justa and Jim wrote daily. They had made up a code so that he could let her know where he would be without putting in information that would be censored. He indicated in some way that he was being sent to Japan and that they needed bolo knives. There were not enough. He didn't have one. Justa didn't even know what one was, but she went up and down State St. and around Chicago with tears in her eyes explaining that her husband was off fighting the Japs single-handedly (as she seemed to really believe), and he had to have a bolo knife. She had all the relatives working on it, and in the end, he had quite an assortment that he really didn't need! However, although he was not a gambler, he shot craps one night and had no money. He put in one of the knives and made $100 that he sent to her. He made very little but spent very little and sent his money to her. She spent none of her earnings except for essentials such as food, room, and transportation. She saved and invested. When the war was over, there was enough money to buy a nice two-story brick house near friends in Park Ridge, Illinois.

CHICAGO TO MADISON

When the Chicago school was functioning well, they needed experienced teachers to help at Truax Field in Madison, Wisconsin. Justa was happy to transfer there. She had served there as camp councilor several years and loved the area. She found a room in a beautiful home on Lake Mendota. She met three nice female instructors, two of whom had suffered from polio and were in leg braces. Justa made friends with them and gave them transportation. When they were on the same shifts. Justa wrote to Jim, "Honey, there are many items rationed. This morning I stopped and left one recapped tire to be recapped again. We are not allowed to buy new tires even though I can't drive these as they are. The casings have to be completely shot or no new tires! I am going to have two tires recapped. Of course, you know that the gas is rationed, but I get coupons because of my job." Justa was living in a room at Mrs. M's. She really mothered the young women who were working at the base. Her son was in service. Justa wrote: "Mrs. M's daughter-in-law is here for a few days with her cute baby. The son is due for a furlough in two weeks. He hasn't seen the baby yet."

JIM WAS NOW AT BARBER'S POINT IN HAWAII

Better an ounce of luck than a pound of gold.
—Yiddish Proverb

Jim was fortunate to be stationed in Hawaii and not in Japan. Although they wrote each day, sometimes there would be no mail, and sometimes there would be a stack of letters all at once. One day when Justa came home there was a huge carton for her in the foyer. There was a little break in the corner with something red sticking out the hole. She couldn't wait to tear into this gift. That red turned out to be the tongue of a big Teddy Bear that she cuddled and loved and took with her on each move. When their daughter Laurie, arrived years later, Teddy was still there. That was her favorite "huggy" for years in spite of many wonderful toys. When Laurie came home one time after she was married, she couldn't believe that her mother had given Teddy away. She was so hooked on him that to this day her home is full of other Teddy Bears, but none has ever been quite the same as that first "huggy".

HAWAIIAN HULA

Justa doing the Hawaiian Hula Holo Holo in Madison, Wisconsin, 1943

Digging down further into the box Justa found a complete genuine Hula costume including the grass skirt, paper bra, lei, anklets, "wristlets", and a book on how to do the Hawaiian hula. There was a silver Hula dancer for her charm bracelet, a sailor doll and everything he could find to buy her. This was special because it was the first box from him since that awful carton came from Camp Peary with his normally immaculate "civies" wadded up in a cake of mud. They were to build that base, and there was nothing there but mud. It was most unpleasant for the men.

Justa had years of satisfaction from the contents of this box. She studied the hula book and then dressed in the hula costume. Patsy, one of her friends who had survived polio and lived with and rode with Justa, took pictures of her at the beach going through all the hip and arm motions. Justa wrote a book called "The Hawaiian Hula a la Madison, Wisconsin". A friend did all the printing and graphics, and the result was sent to Jim and his buddies at Barber's Point in Hawaii.

About thirty years later when Justa was chairperson for a social event at the El Conquistador Country Club in Bradenton, Florida, they had a luau. She got out her hula book, used the English and Hawaiian terms and her usual humor and taught the whole group how to do the hula. She had arranged ahead of time with some of the men to agree to participate. When she invited volunteers, these men came out in their costumes grinning from ear to ear. They rolled their hips and went through the motions as she led them. They were good sports. Then others joined in until almost everyone in the room was involved. They had a great time. It was so popular that she was asked to repeat it at their dance club at the Bradenton Country Club the next year. It was also pleasantly received there with cooperation of dance club members.

THE SEASONS IN MADISON

Living in Madison in that nice home was delightful in the summertime. However, there was a problem. The area where Justa parked her car was also where an ROTC group had to do their morning exercise. If she was on the early shift, she had to get her car out of there before the men started. It became necessary to move to a different neighborhood. Fortunately she was able to find another home on water. This time it was on Lake Monona, but she had to park on the street, and winter was coming with its heavy snowstorms. Often when it was time to start for work, it was dark outside. There was snow piled high on the car. She had to scrape as much as 12 inches off the roof and also dig out the wheels. The job was pretty much hers. Two of her friends had had polio and wore leg braces. Madison did quite a good job of clearing most roads, but it was easy enough to slip, slide, or get stuck. When she didn't have a full car, she still picked up hitchhikers.

One dark, cold morning, the car wouldn't start. The battery appeared to be dead. There was only one other car in sight. It was parked across the street. She stood out in that freezing weather and tried to talk to the two occupants, but they didn't seem to understand. She'd always been good at pantomime, and she thought they understood, but they weren't talking to her. Then she realized that they were deaf mutes. She tried to figure out what to do next. Fortunately another car came by. She flagged down the driver, turned on her smile and sad eyes, had a jump for her battery, and got four instructors to Truax Field on time.

NAVAL SEABEE RETURNS FROM WAR

In 1945 Jim was finally returning from Guam. He was to have a month's leave before taking off for Japan. He had been in the Pacific for so long that Justa was determined to meet him at the train. Her only brother was getting married to a lovely girl. The big formal wedding was all planned. Justa was to be one of the attendants. She had purchased her bridesmaid's dress and slippers. She had to make a choice between the two most important young men in her life, but there was no question of what she would do. She asked to be relieved from the AAF to have this time with her husband, called her brother and sister-in-law-to-be in Rochester, New York and prepared for the reunion with her husband. She met his train in Aurora, Illinois. It was loaded with GI's who were leaning out the windows and whistling at the young ladies. When he finally arrived and she showed up in her honeymoon suit, he said, "Oh, honey, I thought you'd have something new by now." She was being romantic digging out that old suit, but he didn't get it. She did have something new.

Her Naval Seabee Finally Returns (chief's uniform)

There is no such thing as an inevitable war. If war comes, it will be from failure of human wisdom.

—Andrew B. Law

ACROSS THE DESERT TO CALIFORNIA

They had a little time to be with their families in Elgin, Illinois. Then Jim was due to report to Camp Parks near Livermore, California. It was wonderful to be back together, and it was a great trip. However, they were driving across the desert without any air conditioning. They only remember the good part of that trip. When they arrived in Livermore, they checked with Traveler's Aid. Once again "there was no room at the inn". The best that they could be offered was a former chicken coop. Yes, that is not a typo. It was a former chicken coop. The owners had cleaned it out and put a bed in there and offered kitchen and toilet privileges in their humble home. Justa and Jim bought some supplies, swept and scrubbed and slept there in the former chicken house that night.

The next morning Jim had to report to Camp Parks. They went into the house to use the bathroom. Then as Justa opened the kitchen cabinet to get a pan to cook some eggs, a mouse jumped out and almost landed on her. She'd never even seen a mouse before. However, they had a good breakfast that they ate in the kitchen. Jim left for the naval base. Justa was alone in a kitchen coop, without a car or phone. She knew no one or when she would see her husband again. Justa borrowed a rake to work on the mess around what she hoped would be her temporary home.

Neighbors were fascinated with the hard working young woman who was cleaning up something that hadn't been touched in years. They told her that those insects that were everywhere were earwigs. She had never even heard of them before, but she was getting rid of them. The homeowners loaned her a hammer, and she designed a dressing table and some end tables that were made out of orange crates. She began to visualize this as a little dollhouse. There were two windows on the front. She could picture some window boxes planted with something, perhaps geraniums. The owners promised to buy the paint if Justa and Jim would paint the "house".

Then Jim returned. Her back was killing her, but she had always been creative, and she had all these ideas about turning their chicken coop home into a dollhouse. She was chattering about buying paint and how cute this would be. He was trying to tell her that Chuck Shoemaker, a young man from Elgin, was at the base. He and his wife had rented a small duplex in Castro Valley. Justa and Jim could rent the other half. She almost cried. He didn't want her working so hard on this project. All she knew was how much she had accomplished, and now he wanted to go someplace where they'd have to start all over. Surely Chuck's place couldn't be much better. However, they drove there. As soon as they saw it they knew it would be fine. It would be wonderful to have such terrific neighbors in their little duplex with their orange crate furniture.

They were in California when the war ended, and Jim was released December 31, 1945. They took time to drive to Seattle to visit Justa's cousin and aunt on her mother's side. They saw school chums. They also visited with her father's half-brother where she met her biological grandmother for the first time. In each case the families gave them tours of the area. They were treated to a Rose Bowl game and everything else they could possibly want to see.

THEN BACK HOME TO ILLINOIS AND FAMILY

Their First Home, a Wonderful Two-story Brick House

And then they took that long drive across country to Illinois again. They bought a beautiful like-new two-story home near Park Ridge where they had good friends. The sellers were so wonderful and wanted "the kids" to have everything. They loved their lives. They fixed up the basement as a nice playroom including piano, ping pong table etc. While putting acoustical ceiling tiles up, Jim accidentally hit a finger and let the hammer fly. It was the only time in their marriage that she ever saw him lose his temper. The hammer hit an area that he had already done. He considered himself disciplined for that temper tantrum when he had to rip out tiles and redo that part. Justa did some creative work with paint and fabric. She hand painted the inside of a china cabinet to go with the Wedgwood dishes. She hand painted one wall in the bathroom with birds and flowers. Justa was an active volunteer. They had such a wonderful social group. However, Jim questioned the future opportunities in his current position. When two good job possibilities came up, the companies interviewed both of them. The man's family situation was considered important. Jim and Justa chose the one that would necessitate a move to Danville, Illinois.

LOVED THEIR HOME BUT JOB ELSEWHERE

Home is where the heart is

—-Pliny the Elder

They hated to give up this wonderful home, but they put it on the market. To their surprise they had a call immediately. A realtor had a couple that was very interested and they wanted to come right over. However, Justa and Jim had guests for dinner, but why not? The house was in perfect order even the kitchen was the way it should be under the circumstances. Everything smelled delicious. The prospects would witness a beautiful table and well dressed owners with their guests. Justa answered the door graciously and told the realtor to take over, and she went back to her dinner guests. The couple checked all floors. When they passed through the dining room, everybody greeted them as old friends. They went on to the basement. Justa said softly to her dinner guests, "I don't think they could afford one room of this house." That shows how much she knew. When they came back upstairs, they left quietly with a polite, "Thank you." Before dessert was finished, the realtor called to say, "Your house is sold. They were so impressed. They love it. They'll pay your price. They want it right away. They have the cash." And that was that.

CHICAGO TO DANVILLE A DIFFERENT STORY

Now they had to locate someplace to live in Danville. They found an unfinished house that they thought they could complete, and it was in a nice neighborhood. But what a shock! The sellers had stripped it. They disconnected the electricity; so no lights were on when Justa and Jim arrived. Every other real estate transaction in their marriage was just the reverse. Sellers had offered to leave extra items. BUT Justa and Jim made the transition quickly. Jim liked the work, but no neighbors called. They attended the St. James United Methodist Church, but it was summertime, and they had no visitors. A man asked Jim to go to the Jaycees with him one evening. Justa was not accustomed to being left out, uninvited. She missed her friends. Jim met folks at work, but she loved people and wasn't meeting anyone.

In the war years, that was different. But this was a new experience for Justa. That evening after he had been gone for a couple hours, she made up her mind that she would not accept this. She got into the car and drove to the Steak and Shake across from the church. She wasn't even hungry, but she nibbled at her sandwich so that it would last a long time. She stayed there until she knew that he would be home wondering where she was. She just sat there refusing to go back to that empty house. When Jim and his new friend returned home and saw that Justa and the car gone, they were frightened. They did not know where to look. When she finally drove up, Justa who never swore said, "I only came to this damn town to be with you, and I assure you I will not spend any more evenings here alone." And she didn't! She just needed to clarify the issue.

They soon met many wonderful people who became lifelong friends. As this is being written in 2006 everything there has changed again. There is a report that all the manufacturing plants have left the area, jobs are scarce, and real estate values have dropped. There's a rumor about Honda. If Honda should have a plant there, it would be a boon to the area and perhaps turn things around for the better.

LANDSCAPING AND DECORATING CHALLENGES

Justa's work was cut out for her. This new house was not only incomplete. The street address was actually on the side of the house. The long front yard was really just a big field. The potential was there, but it would take creativity, but then she had that. Justa talked the town officials into dumping every kind of excess soil and clippings and junk there to fill what was to become the front yard. Justa and Jim shoveled and raked and leveled. The long porch was about five feet higher than the field. After the area was tall enough, they had good topsoil brought in, and they both worked spreading this. Mr. Harris, the popular local landscaper that everyone in the area was waiting for, was fascinated with this hard working young couple. He'd stop and talk to them, and he warned them that he really didn't think that grass would grow "in that stuff". Justa was determined to prove him wrong. They spread good grass seed and fertilizer, and they kept the area wet. It was sunny weather. They soon had a beautiful lawn. They were able to get some nice rocks that nobody wanted, and they created a lovely rock garden at the narrow end of the house away from the street.

On the back they built a nice patio with free bricks that were left when a former grocery store was torn down. The town finally cut the road through the field on what became the front of the house. Justa planted loads of petunias and such and daily pinched off the dead flowers. Soon people were driving by in amazement and admiration. More came after a reporter and photographer visited and did an article for the local paper. They were celebrities. Mr. Harris came by to check their progress and found Justa painting the garage. He stopped, parked his truck, and came over and took the brush from her and said, "This is the right way to do this—not that." He asked her to sit down, and people watched in amazement as he finished Justa's paint job while they waited for him to do their landscaping work. Justa and Jim painted the ceiling of the 15 x 30-foot living room. They swore they would never do that again! Then Justa made lined floor-length draperies of a beautiful but slippery material. It was all lovely, but she wasn't going to do that again either.

House as They Bought it

House after They worked on it

ST. JAMES UNITED METHODIST CHURCH

They were soon active in the St. James United Methodist Church. However, it didn't have a special circle for the younger ladies. Mrs. Dale, one of the older members, asked if Justa would organize such a circle. She did. It was successful and she served for several years as its chairperson. She was usually a very optimistic individual. One day she was walking down the church corridor feeling a little discouraged with the all the work and little help. There was suddenly an arm around her shoulder. Mrs. Dale came up behind her and said the words that have helped Justa for years,

"If you want to avoid criticism, don't say anything, don't do anything, and don't be anything. You are doing a wonderful job. Keep it up".

Then Justa remembered something that she learned from her parents when she was very young. She overheard the adults at a meeting at their house talking about the man who was the head of the Sunday School Department. That was at the Epworth Methodist Church in Elgin, Illinois. Members really wanted to replace him, but he thought he was indispensable, and they didn't want to hurt his feelings. Did that apply to her now? She decided that it was time for a new chairperson. They asked her to stay on, but she thought it was time for a change. They had a party for her with lots of compliments and a nice gift. She supported the new officers, and all went well. Jim took on every job in the church at one time or another. He was treasurer, pastor parish chairman, and chairman of the board. That meant more work for her because they had always been a team. When one took on a job, the other helped. One time when Jim had an out-of-town meeting, he was late returning for an International Fellowship Club meeting. He was president, but once again, actually they both were. Justa wrote his speech, and he got home in time for her to read it to him and to coach him on what words to emphasize. After he spoke that evening, there were many compliments, but the one that Justa has always remembered with delight was from a woman who came to her and said,

"That husband of yours is certainly a wordsmith. How he can put words together! Aren't you proud of him?" She said, *"Thank you very much."* She refrained from saying, *"Of course, I am. He spoke exactly as I wrote it."*

ADOPTED BUT THEIR VERY OWN CHILDREN

Justa and Jim had wanted four children, but initially they thought they should mature themselves before they started a family. Then the war interrupted. When they were settled and ready to start their family, nothing happened. Then the doctor said, *"You will not be able to have babies with your own genes probably because of Jim's service in the Pacific."* That didn't depress them too much because Justa's father was adopted, and she assumed that they too could adopt. They didn't think that they were especially handsome or brilliant, and there were children who needed homes. Justa had been popular with the children as a camp councilor and assumed that she could handle the mother job. They were both college graduates and had served in the war effort. They were active volunteers and involved in the community. Jim was highly respected and successful in his job and had received his MBA before the war. They were well liked, but there were waiting lists for babies. They contacted adoption agencies including the Children's Home and Aid Society in Chicago where Justa's father and siblings had been left so many years before. They had been to the Cradle in Evanston where Jim had attended college and the Babyfold in Bloomington, Illinois and other agencies. In each case they were accepted but put on a waiting list. Finally in November, 1949 after what seemed an eternity to them, they received a message from the Babyfold. *"We have a beautiful blue-eyed blonde baby girl for you. "*

"Not flesh of my flesh nor bone of my bone, but still miraculously my own." Never forget for a single minute that you didn't grow under my heart but in it."

—Fleur Conkling Heyliger

LAURIE'S ARRIVAL AND JUSTA'S FIRST CRIME

They had waited years rather than the usual nine months, but now it was such a surprise to suddenly "give birth". They had prepared a beautiful nursery long ago with the baby crib and chest of drawers and a rocker for Justa. They had covered a small couch in a clown pattern. The baby's initials were to be LAM; so they had cute pictures of lambs pasted to plywood and cut around and applied to the furniture; so it was a lamb nursery. The room was all set, but suddenly the enormity of what they were undertaking hit Justa. She had read all the baby books and had lists of all the essentials, but she was a perfectionist; so she was out bright and early with her shopping list. Finally she had made all her purchases and headed for her home. She was loaded down when she reached her car and saw that awful parking ticket. What a time for such a terrible thing to happen! She was not used to being a bad girl. She now was guilty of over parking. She had never received a ticket before. With arms full of packages, head full of to-do lists, she rushed into the police station, grasping the ticket and acting as if she'd committed her first murder. Stuttering, stammering, she sputtered, "Officer, this is the first ticket I've ever had and". Accustomed to all the excuses, he responded sarcastically, "I know, you were just a minute late, and". Justa cried out,

"Oh, no, officer, but I just found out yesterday that I'm going to have a baby, and I'm going to have her tomorrow."

The officer looked at her, shrugged his shoulders, tore up the ticket, and said, "You win, lady. That's the best one I've heard yet." He was wide-eyed as she rambled on about her exciting news. When she finally stopped talking and he could get in a word, he grinned, wished her well and sent her on her way. If she'd stayed any longer, he was afraid he might offer to have a baby shower for her. Justa had enough supplies for a nursery full of babies.

The adoption agency was right about one thing. That was the most beautiful baby they had ever seen. However, her eyes weren't blue. She wasn't blonde. She was bald. She was almost five months old. When she finally did grow hair, it was lovely dark brown. Her eyes were gorgeous, huge, sparkling hazel eyes. When Jim sat in his lounge chair and Justa handed the dear little package to him, he held her lovingly, and said, *"You're our little girl now."* She gave him a bright smile as though to say, **"I know that. I'm** here now. Everything will be fine. What are you worrying about?" And she immediately took charge.

JUSTA MOTHER

Justa gave her the first swimming lesson on day one. When she bathed her baby in what they called the "bath table", Justa moved the legs up and down as in a flutter kick and explained about swimming. Then she dried her, put on that wonderful smelling baby powder, and fresh sleepers. She would sing many different songs to her including some of those silly camp songs as she rocked her. Then she'd read out loud anything Justa herself enjoyed. When the first caseworker came from the Babyfold to see how things were going, she said everything looked wonderful. Then she picked up the top book on the table by the rocker and with a strange look asked,

"Is ***this*** *what you read to the baby?* Justa smiled and said, *"Oh, yes, I read everything to her."* It happened to be a book on electronics.

It was not customary reading for most people in 1949. The caseworker obviously thought that that was a little weird. However, Justa has never regretted it. That baby turned into a voracious reader and is knowledgeable on a great many subjects. Justa herself became a "Great Books" leader.

The children were told from an early age that they were adopted. Their birth mothers were just not able to take care of them but wanted them to have good homes. Their adoptive parents wanted them very much and adored them, and were the best parents they knew how to be. Sometimes others were unkind and would say something like, "She not your REAL mother" or "He's not your REAL father". This hurt the children. When they were older, Justa told them that she would do anything in the world that would make their lives better. That included helping them locate their biological parents if they wanted that. Neither of them did until Laurie had her baby. Then because of some health problems she wanted to know more about her genetic background. The agency and the state would not help her. With a little information Justa gave her, she with her own brain and drive was able to find, meet her mother and sisters, and share stories and gifts. They were delighted to meet her and find out that she had a loving family. She was angry that complete strangers had had the history that was so important to her but had not helped her. After that one meeting, she was satisfied and never saw them again.

Then Wes decided that he too would like to know his background. He asked the Cradle but was turned down. Justa then contacted the Cradle and told them that she thought it might really help him, and it certainly was fine with her and Jim. The ladies at the Cradle then were very cooperative and had talks with the family, and it was decided to let Wes think that his request was answered. In some ways Justa really wanted to talk with the birth mother so that each would realize that the other wanted and did what they thought was best for him. He went to see her and stayed quite awhile. She had a big party, and he met lots of relatives and was treated very nicely. She explained that she wanted to keep him, but her mother wouldn't let her. Then suddenly he was home again. In both cases the children said, "You are my parents, my only mother and father." Actually adopted children often feel that there was something bad about them and so they were given away. That's so sad.

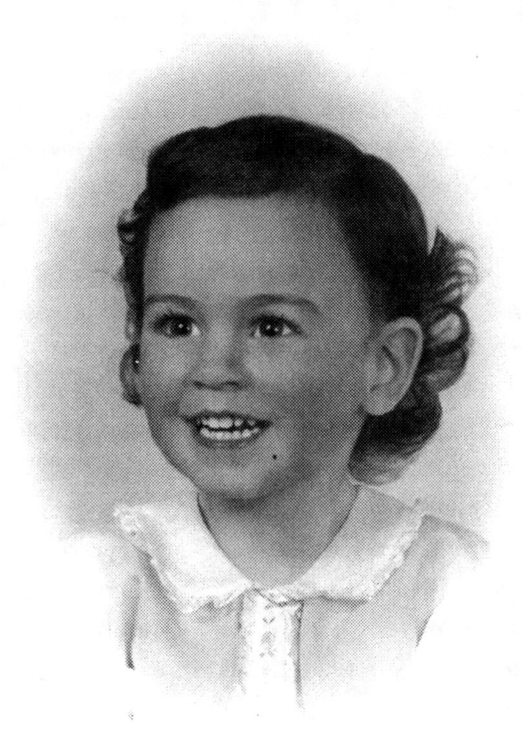

Beautiful little Laurie

TAKING LITTLE LAURIE TO FLORIDA

It was 1952 when the little one had turned into a toddler. Justa and Jim had planned to take a trip to Florida with five other couples. There were no reservations, but all six families would drive to Sarasota and see what they could find. On a Friday afternoon when they were all packed and ready to leave, Jim called from the office. He had been negotiating the union contract with the factory workers. He said that he had not been able to get the union to sign the contract, and he would not be able to leave until the job was done. He didn't want Justa and the little one to be disappointed; so he told her to go on ahead of him and he would come as soon as he could. Justa called their friends who agreed that they would find a place for all and notify the police department. Justa got train tickets and took off with her little girl not knowing where they would stay or if there would be any place.

When they arrived in Sarasota at the train station, Justa and toddler took a cab to the police station. This didn't phase her. She felt that she had had that police experience when she got the parking ticket. The man at the desk looked surprised to see this duo with luggage. Justa started, "Do you happen to have a message", but before she could finish her question, the officer was shaking his head which looked like a "no". In reality it was in disbelief. He said, "I've just had a call from one of your friends who said you would be coming in now. He gave this number and said to tell you that they have rented six cottages in a row at Edgewater Beach Cottages on Longboat Key. We'll call him, and one of them will come in and pick you up." That was what happened. The men at the station acted like hosts and entertained the females until their friends arrived. Jim got the union contract signed, finished his work drove down from Illinois to Florida and joined the others a couple days later. The owners of the place treated the group like family and had cookouts on that beautiful beach. They swam and played in the waves, and built sandcastles. The group returned to the same spot for a number of years while the men were still employed. Justa and Jim then retired in the area.

MERINGUE A LA COMMODE

At age seven, Laurie realized one morning that nothing had been planned for her mother's birthday, and birthdays were big items in this family. On her second birthday she had wanted balloons. When she awakened from her nap, the living room was full of balloons, and she started screaming "Boons, boons, boons". During her whole life she hasn't had a birthday without "boons". So now she couldn't believe that no one had planned a party for Mommy. She took it upon herself to call her mother's friends and invite them to a party. This was an early indication of what a take charge person they had adopted.

Without any adults realizing what she was up to, she mixed up meringue as her mother had done! She had the large cookie sheet in her hands when the doorbell rang. This was a big house. She wanted to get to the door before her mother did. Without putting down her masterpiece she dashed from kitchen, through the dining room and entryway to the lower foyer. At the door she did a quick right into the powder room and laid the meringue tray on the toilet seat.

Then she opened the door and welcomed the guests. They didn't know a little child would take over like this; so they brought the birthday cake. She was quite put out because it was her party. Justa was so surprised. Laurie brought the ladies into the living room and completely neglected the Meringue a la Commode. Justa wasn't a coffee drinker, but her friends were; so Laurie made sure there was coffee. Part way through the event a good friend asked Justa if there were any more coffee. She replied, *"Oh, yes, of course,* The friend replied, *"I don't mean that. I mean coffee grounds. I'll make it. We've been pouring it on the potted plants."* To this day Justa doesn't know if she or Laurie made the coffee. She just subconsciously thinks she can't; so someone else always has to do it. She just says, *"I don't do windows. I don't do coffee."* Of course, she really thinks she can do absolutely anything that she wants to do, but there are certain things that she certainly has no intention of doing.

JUSTA CAN FIND HUMOR IN ALMOST ANYTHING BUT SOME THINGS JUST AREN'T FUNNY

Probably Justa's best quality is her dry sense of humor. She has so often heard, "I love to be with you. You are so funny." She says that it's the best medicine she has found. Justa never really thought of herself as "just a" something; so it would bother her a little when a reporter would write something impressive about her and then identify her as a housewife and/or Jim's wife. She knew that she was successful in many realms; so why did this term offend her? They didn't call Jim just an office husband. Once she overheard two men talking about her. One said to the other, *"It's a pity to waste a brain like that on a housewife."* The other man agreed. She couldn't believe how little they understood. Being a homemaker not only takes energy and intelligence but every possible skill and virtue if she is to do the job properly.

HAD WANTED FOUR CHILDREN NOW HAD TWO WESLEY GLENN NAMED AFTER TWO UNCLES

Their dear little boy named Wes

They had always planned to have four children, but life had changed that for them. They did want their daughter to have siblings to grow up with, but she was an only child for five years because there was a long wait for that to occur. They were very happy when the Cradle called to say that they had a baby boy for them. When Wes arrived, his big sister put on her mother's gray lady hat and a mask to keep any germs from the baby. Wes cried a lot, and the parents and pediatrician could not determine why. He was getting the same treatment as the first baby. They did not learn until he was almost middle-aged that the birth mother may have been a drinker. Doctor indicated that he might have suffered from fetal alcohol syndrome. Wes was a sweet little boy and trained to be courteous and polite. In first grade some boys laughed at him when he held the door open for the ladies. He was hyperactive and found it hard to sit still. Therefore, he had trouble sitting through long intelligence tests, and the results did not show his actual intelligence correctly. He was jumping around in line one day, and a male teacher took him to the principal and said that he was going to beat him. She objected, but the male abused the child with a two by four. The parents did not know this until he was a man in his forties. At that time at least in that school nothing was done about hyperactivity.

BOTH CHILDREN WERE WONDERFUL AND HAD MANY SUCCESSES AND PROBLEMS TOO

Wes liked magic; and he was good with tricks; so Justa bought every magic trick she could find mostly from Marshall Fields. She had cut down the formal "tails" that Jim had worn and had a top hat for him. He was cute, good, and in demand to entertain family, neighbors, and friends. Jerry and Dick Van Dyke were from the same town. One of the boys had worked in the factory that Jim managed. Their father, Cookie, was a salesman who called on Jim. He was really ridiculously funny. One day when he was working in their yard, a woman came by and complimented him and not knowing who he was, asked if he'd work for her and what his rates were. He is reputed to have said "yes" and that she could have the same deal as the lady of this house. She slept with him.

Justa loved the pantomime comedy that Jerry and Dick did and so she arranged with their pantomime coach, Tex Cromwell, to teach Wes. He and three other little boys made up a foursome that was very funny. When they entertained, they usually wore red and white striped jackets and hats and their acts brought more laughter and joy to Justa than any of his many trophies. He didn't stay with it. There were too many activities for the youngsters. He stayed with scouting until making his Eagle badge. When he had trouble with earning several badges, Justa worked with him until they were perfect. Justa helped him with his first speech for the student council and created a campaign picture for him. She drew a little freckled face and had the words, "Don't Guess, Vote Wes". He was well liked. He won. He served. Wes excelled in swimming from a young age. Laurie was on the sidelines cheering him on in his early competition. When he was seven, he won the trophy for most improved swimming in his age group, and from then on, his name was almost always first for each stroke, and he was anchor man for the relay teams. His room was full of ribbons, medals, and cups. This brought him popularity with the kids but later jealousy. He received a scholarship to the University of Georgia and was a varsity swimmer as a freshman.

Wes was a magician

Junior Olympian Champion,

Table full of Wes' trophies

Eagle Scout with Scoutmaster"

LAURIE AT SUMMER CAMP

Justa had enjoyed her childhood years at summer camp. It was such a valuable part of her growing up. She wanted her children to have those experiences. When they arranged for Laurie to go to camp in Minnesota, she later said that she had felt they wanted to get rid of her. But how she loved it and wanted to return each year! She became good at horsemanship, canoeing, sailing, and theater arts, and she developed a great love of nature. As an adult she was such a good friend and almost a family member of camp's owner. When she could afford it, she bought a small piece of property near camp with her own little lake that she planned to build on someday. She just loves getting off into the woods and sitting by the campfire. When Wes went off to summer camp, he got into mischief double-sheeting other camper's beds and having pans of water over the entrance to a tent and rigged so that it would dump water on the camper entering. Perhaps Justa played some of those tricks at camp too, and yet she was chosen "Indian Princess" which meant outstanding camper.

LAURIE'S ALLERGIES

Laurie had an earache problem that doctors couldn't solve. She would have the pain that was caused by infection. But she seemed to be allergic to the antibiotics given to cure that. Justa took her to see a famous specialist whose office was high up in a skyscraper in Chicago. They had to be there fairly early in the morning, and the tests took to almost noon. The doctor suggested that they go down to the ground floor to a little restaurant and have some lunch before he discussed the results. They were hungry; so that was good. Laurie asked if she could have a chocolate milk shake. Justa, still new to this problem answered, "I don't know why not, honey." This disappeared very quickly, and the child asked if she might have another of the same. It had been a difficult morning for her; so Justa responded, "Well, I think that would be all right."

DOCTOR'S INSTRUCTIONS

After their little lunch, they took the elevator up to that office that exuded success. The doctor greeted them kindly as they sat opposite him at that impressive desk. He sat leaning forward with his chin on his hands, looked into Justa's eyes and said, *"Now Mother, this is what I would like you to do. I want you to take this child off of all chocolate, all cow's milk, wheat, and bread. The bird, cat, dog, carpeting, draperies must go. The mattress because it has sisal grass must go."* Basically he was telling this little girl and her loving mother that she was allergic to life. They had to search for a place to buy goat's milk and bread with no ingredients. To put it simply, it would take a book just to list the limitations put on their household. It was years later that Laurie thought that she had overcome her allergies, but Justa never thought so.

The other grandmother of her only grandson said that Laurie was an enigma. Justa often analyzed that. As an adult Laurie suffers with fibromyalgia and weak bones with so much pain. Justa thought it interesting when Dr. Donohue wrote a column (April, 2006) describing fibromyalgia as an enigmatic disease. The dictionary defines an enigma as a puzzling thing or person. It's true that the disease is hard to define. There is so much pain but no explanation of the cause or cure. Laurie is so bright, beautiful, caring, and capable, but she can only function for several hours a day. She can not stand or sit for any length of time.

Laurie was a good swimmer and diver but did not like competition. Justa would rather dance than anything, and although her daughter had dancing lessons, she didn't really seem to enjoy it. Report cards would say that she was not living up to her potential. She was bored. The program was not stimulating enough for her. Her parents gave her the opportunity to attend prep school so she might get more individual attention. They chose the Elgin Academy in Elgin, Illinois because her grandparents lived there, and she would feel close to family. Laurie had biological sisters who were not put up for adoption. The birth mother just couldn't take care of her. She had whooping cough before she arrived and eczema on arrival and other health problems.

Dancing with Great-grandson first time

Dancing with great-grandson improved

OTHER MEMORIES OF THEIR CHILDHOOD

When Wes was small he said, *"You know who I mean, Mommy. The man with the wrinkled hair!"* Laurie left footprints on the kitchen counter when she was trying to find the candy bars that she was not supposed to eat and Justa had hidden. Cousin Eric left the dinner table, went upstairs, and when he returned, he had a head that looked like the Indians had scalped him. He'd found the razor that Jim had used to trim Wes' hair and had used it on his own head. Justa was reminded of how upset her mother had been when her Dad was baby sitting her, and she crawled under the table where her Dad was doing paper work and she cut off her beautiful curls. Also there is the story of her Dad's curls which his mother and then Laura had carefully saved in a lock box. That box was stolen by burglars and then found out behind the garage where the thief had opened it searched for valuables and left John's baby curls. Justa still has all the curls. John's have been in Laura's gold engraved locket from 1915. Laura gave it to Justa when she was a freshman in college. Justa has now given it to Laurie. Apparently a baby's curls don't take priority when a thief needs money for food and lodging.

WHO IS THE WITCH?

On Halloweens Justa wouldn't let the children go out alone to trick or treat. So she donned a black costume, a long black wig and a witch's pointed hat. When the children went to the doors to trick or treat, Justa rode a broom as she danced around the front yards. For several years there was one man in the neighborhood that was determined to find out which child came as the witch. He didn't recognize his own neighbor.

FOREIGN STUDENTS

1961 Justa and Jim had opened their lovely home to foreign students whom they treated as their own children. It not only helped the students, but it was a learning experience for the whole family. This time when they were told that their guest would be a young man from South Africa, they had no clue what this would mean. When they drove to the gathering spot where hosts picked up their guests-to-be, a handsome white male came up to them smiling and saying, *"I am Charles de Haas. Did you expect me to be black?"* They just smiled back. It would not have mattered. They would just accept the one who came. This was fun and educational for all. A committee had made all the arrangements for tours. Jim usually gave them a special tour of the Chuckles Candy Co. Justa accepted them into the family and fed them the same food. They played games together and asked about their families at home and their country. Their stories were interesting.

Charles' family had a large ranch in the Belgian Congo, an African country where there was trouble. They had to get out, and they moved to South Africa. Justa never told me the whole story. He visited them several other times including the year that Brian Adlam was their guest from Weymouth, England. The boys got along well. When Brian married, he tried to bring his bride to their home for a visit, but they were unable to schedule a mutually satisfactory time. When Charles was married in a big wedding in Paris, he wrote a beautiful personal letter inviting them. Of course, the bride's family sent them the formal invitation. They also received a formal invitation from a princess who was having a special party for the bride and groom. Justa would have been thrilled to make the trip to meet his family and friends in Paris. At that time her French was still fairly good. He was such a nice young man, and everything would have been spectacular, but Jim felt that it would be hard to leave the children and the factory. The last time they heard from Charles the letter came on fine stationary, and at the top it said Charles De Haas, Director of the World Wildlife Association. He would do something that would help society.

ALADDIN WITH IRAQI EMBASSY A TOUR IN WASHINGTON

Their next guest was Aladdin Aljabouri, a graduate student at the University of Chicago. His home was in Iraq, and he was a Muslim. The whole family asked him many questions about food, religion, language, housing, and customs. Aladdin wrote out answers for Laurie and Wes. Justa suggested that particular sheet be included in this story. He gave her a book about his country, but that was 45 years ago. She doesn't remember anything about Sunni or Shiite to try to understand the Middle East now. When Aladdin finished his graduate studies, he was sent to Washington D. C. to serve as an attaché at the Iraqi Embassy.

When there was a confectioner's convention in Washington that they were planning to attend, Justa notified Aladdin. He was eager to see them and offered to be her tour guide in Washington. He was proud to say that he would have his embassy car. Jim went to meetings. The embassy car picked up Justa at the hotel, and her tour began. Even though she had been to Washington several times before, she saw things from a different perspective. He was a gracious host and took her into the embassy and introduced her to all the officials. The last message she had from him came from the Iraqi Embassy in Pakistan where he was stationed. He had married an Iraqi doctor. Justa has wondered so often what has happened to him and his family with all the horrors that have gone on in his country so many years later. He would probably be a grandfather. She hopes that he and his family are safe and well, but she doesn't know. His children or grandchildren could be in this mess, or they could all have moved elsewhere.

ENTERTAIN UNITED NATIONS DELEGATES

In 1962 Justa and Jim were asked to host one of the eight United Nations delegates who would be visiting Danville. Jim had been president of the United Nations local group. They were told that their houseguest would be the delegate from Syria. Justa read and studied to learn what she could to better understand that country and their guest. At the last minute plans were changed, and their visitor was Geza Selmeci representing the Permanent Mission of the Hungarian People's Republic. They picked him up and accepted him as they had their foreign students. He stayed in their home for several days. Almost immediately he and Wes were outside playing catch with a ball that Geza brought and autographed for the child. A little later a deputy showed up at the front door. He apologized for disturbing her but wanted her to understand what was going on. There had been quite a political upheaval in Hungary. Some Hungarians had escaped that government and were now living in Danville. It was said that they wanted to blow up the house of these people (Justa and Jim) who were entertaining the enemy. They lived on a large curve in a lovely wooded area. Without making a big show, there would be a squad car parked on the curve to protect them as long as these guests were in town. Well, this added a new dimension to their plans.

However, nothing was disrupted in the days spent seeing power plants, factories, and university. All eight of the guests seemed to thoroughly enjoy all the activities and they said that this visit gave them an entirely different opinion of the United States. They said that it was so different from New York and Washington. Especially they liked the people so much more. Perhaps visiting foreign diplomats should have the opportunity to spend time with ordinary citizens more often.

One day Justa served a nice luncheon in her formal dining room for Geza Selmici from Hungary and Mehdi Ehsassi from Iran, Jean-Baptiste Tapsoba from Upper Volta who was dressed in his colorful native garb, and Chi-Min Wei from the Republic of China. There was a maid's bell under the carpet by her chair that she just had to touch with her foot, but she did almost everything herself. Then she took them in her car to Champaign/Urbana to see the University of Illinois. The university had experts giving tours of everything. They were especially interested in the model farm. She enjoyed listening to their conversations about the world. She remembers vividly when one of the four questioned another, "Are you going to ask for money from the United States?" If that question were asked today, Justa would have thought, *"Why not? Doesn't everybody?"* She was sufficiently busy being a hostess that unaccustomed as she is to being quiet and listening, that was what she did.

Their home for 20 years where they entertained and raised their children

Their home - 30 years later

SORRY, SENORA, NO ROOMS AT THE INN

It was a last minute decision, but Justa decided that the whole family could stand a vacation. The children would be on Christmas holiday from school, and Jim said he could get away. Justa made arrangements with Cook's Travel for airline tickets to Mexico City and a guide and a driver from there to Taxco, Cuernavaca, and on to Acapulco with stops in between. The agent couldn't confirm anything definite in Acapulco because it was so busy at the holiday time, but Justa said, "Set up what you can." The agent did. They saw what they could in Mexico City and surrounding areas. Justa's cousin, Mike, worked at the embassy and had recommended Belmonico for a restaurant. It was good. One of the most troubling things that Justa saw was a poor woman on her knees moving forward a long distance with her gift to give at the Shrine of Guadeloupe. It seemed so wrong. She should have been on the receiving end, not having to be on her knees giving.

They wanted to go on with their plans but were reassured that there was no place to stay in Acapulco. There was a driver dressed nicely in "livery" and looking very professional standing nearby. He introduced himself as

Eduardo and said that his best friend was manager of the nicest resort down there and that he could guarantee accommodations for the family in Acapulco. Justa cancelled the rest of the Cook agreement and took off with the replacement chauffeur /guide. Their young son sat up in front with Eduardo and practiced and improved his Spanish. There were many questions asked and answered, and every place on the way South was investigated. It was delightful.

They had a couple of nights in Taxco, the silver capital, and they spent Grandmother's Christmas gift money on jewelry. When they finally arrived in Acapulco, the driver pulled up to a beautiful resort hotel, took them to a table by the pool and said, *"Now just relax and swim, have a drink or just watch the children swim while I make the arrangements."* He returned shortly. He'd taken off his hat because it was hot, and he was getting hotter. He said, *"Oh, Senora, I'm so sorry, but there is no room at the resort, but no problem. I have another friend, a nice place. I will be right back."* He soon returned. This time he was without his coat, and he was covered with perspiration. After about a half dozen of these *"Senora, I'm so sorry "* reports, each time with one less garment, Justa was getting the picture, "*There is no room at the inn.*" In the meantime they had seen the boys dive for coins from the high rocks at La Perla and everything else there was to see in the area. Justa had developed a fondness for Eduardo who was like one of their exaggerating kids, and she really didn't mind when he said, "*Oh, Senora, Cuernavaca is a lovely town. Would you mind if we drive back there? I will call.*" He did.

You already know the answer. There was a big convention there, and right! There was no room at the inn. They had quite a creative young man here though. "*Senora, would you mind staying in a private home if the owners move out*?" Justa laughed and replied, "*Only if you stay with us.*" So off he went in search of Mexicans in a nice home who would find his story interesting enough to move out for several days. Justa had already found this vacation different and fun, and somehow she knew that he would find a stable or something! She and Jim and young Wes had wandered off when they were in Mexico City, and when they needed help, Justa asked, "*Donde esta Calle Juarez*?" Somehow it didn't translate to "*Where is Juarez St.?*" Finally Justa had tried a question with the word hotel in it, and the response was immediate. "*Oh, si, si, Hotel Hilton!*" Well, no, they were not staying at a Hilton, but they knew where that was; so it saved them. This time they would keep their translator with them. Eduardo had found a nice home. Justa's family had their own bedrooms, and Eduardo had his. There was a good kitchen, but they preferred the fine restaurants that were available. A good time was had by all. It was fun for Eduardo too. He was proud of his success.

ABOUT WES GOOD BUT SAD

Wes was on the student council. He was an Eagle Scout. He won a scholarship to the University of Georgia and swam with the team as a freshman and sophomore. His parents didn't know that he was drinking or that he had a serious problem. He came home at Christmas time his sophomore year. He just wasn't himself, but he had lovely presents for them. For Justa he had chosen a special Readers Digest Songbook of Western Country Music. She had the other Readers Digest Songbooks, but she had never thought of this one. It broke Justa's heart to see him in this condition. They took him to many doctors, but they never did get satisfactory help. They just said, "Your son is very ill." The so-called therapists actually did harm by putting ideas into his head of things that never happened. It was years later before he explained the alcohol problem to them. He stayed without alcohol for the rest of his life thanks to AA. His main goal in life was to help others. He couldn't come into the house without some flowers or a gift for his mother. One day he purchased a wet suit for himself and so also one for Justa. It was quite a sight for the neighbors when she showed up at the pool with her new gift. His life ended at age 50 due to a ruptured aneurysm.

Justa and Jim loved the children so much but didn't realize until years later that part of their problems were that they were trying so hard to please their parents. They both grew up trying to help other people, especially their parents who weren't aware of the sibling rivalry going on. Laurie was an only child for five years, and then when she was off to camp and school, Wes was an only child. Justa was always impressed with her younger sister-in-law, Barbie, who had eight children. Of course, they had problems, but she kept lists of their jobs on the refrigerator. They could see they all had work to do and were treated equally.

JUSTA ENJOYED CREATIVE WORK

During the most difficult times with the children Justa did creative work. She kept two easels up. The one was for the oil paintings. She really tried to do portraits, but they were not satisfactory. Therefore she turned them into clowns and became quite adept at those. Once again her sense of humor came into play. On the other easel she had a huge sketchpad and did charcoal drawings of the people in the news. She would study the covers of magazines such as Time and Life and then do her own variation of the heroes, criminals and politicians. She did many at the time of President Kennedy's murder. It was great therapy.

She also wrote skits and prepared posters for any organization she was in. She taught country club children water ballet, wrote the programs and prepared the music, and assigned costumes, lighting, and other jobs to parents. She wrote articles on antiques and auction sales for the Tri-State Trader. For the Danville Symphony Board she created the auction book all in rhyme. For the Danville Country Club she created invitations to all the events once she was told who, what, when and a theme. For her PEO Sisterhood each year she prepared skits for Founder's Day just taking themes such as the Bolshoi Ballet or hippie days. Her sisters played the parts in the appropriate costumes. When she studied history, she tried to associate family members back as far as she could. That helped her not only learn the history but be able to picture the descendents in that clothing and that housing and that transportation.

JUSTA WAS NO UGLY AMERICAN BUT JIM DIDN'T WANT TO GO THIS TIME

You have never seen the word "no-ugly" before? Well, that is because Justa created the word and has never shared it with others until now. She wanted to be sure that she was never an ugly American. She always smiled, tried their language, and made an effort to be pleasant and helpful and let other people help her. In 1967 when Justa suggested to Jim that they go to Europe, he said, "*Oh, I couldn't leave the factory that long.*" Justa replied, "*Oh, I think you could.*" He did, and he never again questioned the trips she continually planned, and they traveled joyously and covered the planet rather thoroughly. It was only when Justa said, "*Well, we've been almost everywhere except Antarctica.*" Before she could relay her ideas, Jim replied, "*And I don't want to go there.*" Justa laughed and thought "*He's pleasantly taken every trip I ever scheduled, and I don't think that he really does want to do this, and I don't have to go there. It is a little cold for him.*"

JUSTA THE LINGUIST IN EUROPE 1967

On that first European trip, Justa had a little advantage in France because she had studied French all through high school and college. In college she had her meals at a French table because students were required to sit at a foreign language table and speak only that language or not eat. In Paris when there was a taxi strike, Justa struck up a conversation in the hotel lobby with a gentleman who no doubt was fascinated with this vivacious young woman who was making such an effort to speak this language but had a funny accent. No doubt his English was much better than her French was. She had heard that the French were unfriendly; so she was pleasantly surprised at his responses. She told him that her group, at her instigation, was planning to go across town to a restaurant named Joseph's that had been highly recommended to Jim. Now with the taxi strike they would have to make other plans. He immediately replied that that would not be necessary. He had a van. He wasn't busy. He would drive the group to the restaurant and wait and bring them back to the hotel or leave and return at the hour they requested. She was trusting enough and a good enough salesperson to convince the others that it would be safe. The Frenchman was a delight and lived up to this word. The only problem was that several people later became ill from the snail delicacy, escargot, that had been highly recommended. After the taxi strike was over, a cab driver realized Justa was really trying to speak the language properly. She hoped she wasn't "too "trying". In any event he helped her with her accent and had some success. They both broke into laughter as she tried and failed continually with the pronunciation of Champs Elysee. To this day she doesn't think it should be "chawns".

Justa used a combination of French and English when she bought a beautiful ensemble from a designer shop in Paris. She even had a coat and shoes and hat to go with it. Then the rains started; so she had to buy an umbrella, but not just any umbrella. It was a work of art with a gold handle with a jewel on top. Of course, she has practically never used it. It looked really elegant in the umbrella stand in the foyer. When they moved to a retirement home, the umbrella stand with all the umbrellas including this piece of "art" disappeared with no explanation from the moving company. There was no way that she could be compensated for this. It was a part of an overall picture designed at that special time. She reported this and the other missing and broken items to the director at Freedom Village. He in turn wrote to the president of the moving company and told him that although they had been recommended for years, he did not want to see any of their trucks on the property ever again. The president called and made an appointment to talk to Justa. He visited her, and they had a long talk about the business and children. Of course, her parents had been in business and she knew it wasn't easy. However, this was really bad. She is a softy and never wants to hurt anybody. She was the only one who could get him out of this and foolishly accepted a tiny cash offer. She didn't really even negotiate with him. She should have been tougher so it would not happen to someone else. But if he didn't have all that business, it could put him under. She didn't want that to happen to him and his family.

FRENCH AROUND HER DINING ROOM TABLE / THE ITALIAN OLD BRIDGE FOR JEWELRY

Now back to 1967. Justa didn't want to give up on French; so when she returned from a European trip, she invited friends who were would-be French speakers to sit around her dining room table once a week and converse on all topics but in one language. The accents varied from Justa's "Chicawgo" to ones from Cuba, Germany, Alsace Lorraine, and others. Olga was the greatest. She could speak many languages, but she'd go from one right into another while the rest were trying to figure out what she had just said in one. She knew her languages but not her grammar. There were pluses to these gatherings. They all learned more than the language, and they had so many laughs. Laughter is such good medicine.

In Rome, Italy they made a special trip to the old bridge so Justa could shop for a friend who had brought a piece of lapis lazuli jewelry there years ago and wanted matching earrings. Justa didn't know what she was doing, but she had brought a magnifying glass with her. When the owner saw that, he came to her immediately and helped her quickly find what she wanted. Then when she looked at cameos, he said, "*Oh, no, Madame, that is not superior enough merchandise for you. I will bring you the most magnificent cameo I have ever had.*" He did, and Justa was convinced, and she has had it on display all these years since. Any other cameo looks so inferior in comparison. He must have really been a great salesman.

QUEEN OF THE RHINE

In 1974 they took a Rhine River Cruise. They visited every community where the boat stopped. They talked to everyone, always throwing in a phrase or two in the appropriate tongue. They made new friends, climbed up to the Melk Monastery and bought an interesting antique iron that she carried home to Illinois. At one point when there was no stop, everyone was given the opportunity to take what he or she wanted from the craft shop and create a hat. That was up Justa's alley. Out of some junk she built forms for hats for Jim and herself. She found an assortment of pretty colored crepe paper that she used to make outstanding hats for Jim and herself. Everyone paraded around. The winner was chosen by applause. She was chosen "Queen of the Rhine". A man from New York tried to convince her that she belonged in his city doing design work.

Queen of the Rhine

ARRIVAL IN RUSSIA 1974-75

They were in Russia for New Year's Eve. Before this trip Justa studied Russian with a Lithuanian woman. This really helped her with all the essentials. Their first hotel was the Rossia in Moscow. They were told that they had to go in and out a particular door. They arrived late at night dressed in fur coats, hats, gloves, and fleece-lined boots. They were tired from their flight but within walking distance of Red Square; so six of them trekked over there in the snow that covered their clothing and made coats seem so heavy. It was fascinating to see St. Basil's and the Kremlin and all, but suddenly they were very tired and had to walk back to the hotel. The hotel took up the whole block. They went in the closest door.

At every turn they were greeted with "Nyet". Even Justa's smile and linguistic endeavors would only let them in that one door and they didn't want to go that far. When they finally got in out of the cold, she saw a marble bench and wanted to lie down on it and find their room in the morning. "Nyet". Well, so much for her language efforts. Each floor of the hotel had heavy-set, stern looking women who were in charge of the room keys that had to be taken out and turned in to them before leaving the floor. All they wanted that first night was to get a key and find a horizontal spot to lie on. They did.

The corridors were long, and it was quite a distance from counter to the room. Each time they came or went Justa tried her Russian on the "floor lady". One day she had to say that the key wouldn't work, or the key was broken. She added her charade talents to her language efforts to make her point and had response from the other side of the counter. She was actually being helped with the pronunciation. She repeated, and then the Russian woman would say it again. Then there was actually a smile, and an arm was extended, and the two walked down to the room, and the door was unlocked. Justa smiled, stepped back and did a curtsy as she said, "*Bolshoi Spaseeba*". That was too much for Justa's new friend who just cracked up, and with tears in her eyes, reached out and hugged Justa and continued to be her helper for the rest of the trip. They were friends.

LOST IN MOSCOW / FRENCH SUPPLY TRANSPORTATION

One day there was nothing scheduled. Justa and Jim roamed about and mingled with the children. They had been told that the kids wanted gum to trade for Russian medals. Jim managed the Chuckles Candy Co. and thinking that he would have something better than "goom" to trade, he brought loads of candy. He was wrong. At first the children didn't know what those wonderful colorful jelly candies were, and negotiating was not that good. However, they still managed to come home with a nice assortment of Russian medals from their trading with the kids. Justa wondered if they dared to go off on their own away from the tourist area. Usually in big cities some people speak English, and if you smile, know a little of their language, and can do charades, you can manage.

Justa asked about those public buses they saw. They got on one, communicated fairly well with the other riders but probably stayed on a little too long. They were certainly beyond any tourist area when they got off. They roamed around and saw more than the others in their group would ever see, but then they tried to find a bus. Nyet, there didn't seem to be any, and they really didn't know where they were. Justa was about to decide that this time maybe she had been a little too adventurous and they had pushed their luck too far when she saw what looked like a tourist bus. She flagged it down, found out that it was a French group. They were happy to let Justa and Jim join them and get them back to their hotel. Her French accent still wasn't perfect, but her efforts helped. Their English was undoubtedly much better than her French anyway.

NEW YEARS EVE IN MOSCOW

On New Year's Eve their group sat at a long table loaded with bottles and fruits. Most people enjoyed the vodka, but Justa wasn't a drinker, and when they opened a bottle that was an arm's length in front of her face, she insisted that it burned her throat. A highlight of that evening was when the public address system was blaring out communist propaganda. The Northwestern University representative, Ray Willeman, leading their group, took a bullhorn, climbed up on the circular staircase, signaled for the group to stand, and they all sang, "God Bless America". Justa felt chills up and down her spine. She suspected that not many communists in the room knew enough English or were sober enough to be too aware of what they were hearing.

It was still cold in their room, but they had been warned about that and their daughter had bought sleepers with feet in them and other warm garments. Each night they bundled up. It wasn't until the day they were checking out that Justa noticed the drapery at the right end wasn't hanging properly, and so good homemaker that she was, she went to straighten it out. A cold breeze hit her, and she knew then for the first time that the reason the room was so cold. They were in Russia, and they had been bathing and dressing and sleeping with the windows open! It wasn't that cold in the hotel. One just had to be smart enough to close the windows!

1995 AMAZON ECOLOGICAL TOUR CELEBRATING THEIR 54TH WEDDING ANNIVERSARY

We live in a wonderful world that is full of beauty, charm and adventure. There is no end to the adventures that we can have if only we seek them with our eyes open.

—Jawaharlal Nehru

When Justa learned that Sarasota's famous Selby Botanical Gardens was sponsoring a trip to the tropical rainforest along the Peruvian Amazon, she just had to go. She knew of Margaret Lowman and her part in canopy walkways and her work at Selby Gardens. The tour would include a walk in the treetops above the rainforest on what was at the time the only canopy walkway in the Americas. It turned out to be a once–in-a-lifetime opportunity. There were two months of preparation, much more than for a trip around the world. They bought purses that would hang around their necks for their passports, health cards, and money. They had been warned about pickpockets in Iquitos, reportedly a miserable place, but the entry point to this fabulous spot. The Sarasota County Health Unit gave them a list of travel tips. "Avoid ice. Drink bottled beverages only. Brush teeth with bottled water. Avoid raw vegetables. Eat only fruit you peel yourself. Avoid fruit salad. Avoid dairy products. Pepto Bismol is an effective diarrhea medication. Take extra supply of prescription medications. Consider taking extra pair of glasses or contact lenses."

They had immunizations for yellow fever and cholera, tetanus and booster gamma globulin. They started anti-malarial pills one week before departure, and would have to take it for four weeks after. They bought sulfur powder to put into shoes and around the waist. To fight off insects they needed 100 % DEET. They took a bag of food supplements and every possible medication. Jim wore his hearing aids. Justa's were new and expensive; so she left them home. They really didn't help her much that way. Jim wore his glasses. Justa hung hers around her neck in case of emergency—for example actually wanting to see something. And then there were the binoculars, water bottles, sunscreen, flashlight, alarm clock, rain gear, knives, and everything but the kitchen sink.

After this exhausting preparation, Justa must have thought she needed one more thing to make this a really auspicious beginning. So—a couple weeks before their departure she developed a viral infection, then laryngitis, and then a bad cough. She had chest pain; so the doctor did an EKG and chest x-ray. Doctor prescribed Daypro for pain. She steamed her nose and throat, took antibiotics which don't help viral infection but might help bacterial. They took care of their family's needs and committee responsibilities. She would not give up this trip after all this preparation. Of course, she was exhausted before starting. Jim's ears seemed worse than ever, and she had to repeat everything three times for him until her voice gave out completely. She finally communicated with Jim by writing notes in a notebook.

They met the other tour participants at the Selby Gardens parking lot. And this is the way they introduced themselves to these strangers who would be like family for the next week. She pointed to her mouth and shook her head indicating that she couldn't talk, to her eyes to mean that they aren't so good either, and to Jim's ears and raised her eyebrows that there might be a little problem communicating. Katy said, "*We're so glad that you are with us.*" Marianne asked the bus driver, "*Do you know how to get to Miami*?" Response was, "*I think so.*" And then, "*I've made the trip at least 28 times.*"

This reminded Justa of Pagan, Burma many years ago when they were on the small plane waiting to depart for Rangoon and heard, "rrhumph, hurrumph" or some such tune. Then the pilot stuck his head in and inquired, "*Are there any engineers on the plane?*"

Justa thought to herself, "I think I'm as close to an engineer as anyone on this plane. If that's the case, we are in trouble." They needed to get to Rangoon and onto their ship, or they would have some unpleasant days. Two men did get up to join the pilot. They soon heard three stronger "hurrumphs", and the helpers hopped back on the plane, and they were off.

FIRST THEY HAD TO GET TO MIAMI

Where was I? Oh, yes, they stopped in Naples, Florida for lunch. Thank goodness that she remembered to mail the $100 check to Red Cross to help those troubled people in Oklahoma City. They were victims of the car bombing of the Federal Building. Justa is always troubled when people do such awful things in the name of religion. On Alligator Alley en route to Miami they saw no alligators although Marianne said that she saw several on a recent trip. Bruce was a nice young man travelling with them. He was a naturalist working at Selby Gardens and had his doctor's degree. He was also bilingual; so his Spanish was good. When disembarking at the airport, he dropped his backpack, and the zipper broke. His wonderful camera fell out, and all lenses were cracked, and he couldn't screw them on.

Before they left, there were newspaper articles about clashes between Peru and Ecuador. Troops were headed for the jungle frontier with Ecuador. Each country blamed the other for the attack. There were reported murders. All the news was negative, but they paid no attention. They were so excited about the potential of this special trip. The only way to get to Iquitos, Peru was by air or the Amazon River. There was only one flight a week by Faucet Air, and some questioned its safety. About that time they read about a Faucet plane that crashed. All of the passengers were killed. Yes, but they were going to the Tropical Rain Forest of Peru, and nothing was going to stop them.

The Selby Gardens group was headed for the Explorama Inn about 25 miles beyond Iquitos. It was the only jungle lodge directly on the Amazon. The river is 40 miles across at its widest. The water level can actually change in depth 45 feet. Justa remembers a bus ride, and other travel by boats and feet. The Explorama Lodge was 50 miles down the Amazon on a tributary. It was in the main rainforest with the highest biodiversity of trees in the world. Scientists study the amazing number of trees, plants, exotic birds, and all the native wildlife.

THEY MADE IT TO PERU AND THE RAIN FOREST

I think that I am correct with these names and numbers, but all I know is what Justa told me. After all she's 88 going on 90 and could possibly make a mistake. But she clearly remembers the night that she slept with a tarantula! Well, she didn't exactly sleep **with** it. I mean that she might have slept if it hadn't been on the wall four feet from the foot of her cot. She watched it all night. She didn't dare go to sleep, for she didn't know what it might be up to. That night they had a door and windows; so it couldn't get out! Of course Jim once again slept on his good ear. I don't know why she'd be concerned about a little creature like a tarantula. It was probably only about six inches in diameter. One day she picked up a baby sloth and held it in her arms as she did her own babies. She's ridden on horses, donkeys, camels, and elephants. She played golf with the alligator. Well, not exactly with, but next to. You can see that she's not exactly consistent in her feelings. Elaine had a lizard fall into her "room".

They had **some** primitive living just as the natives. There they had palm thatched individual cottages. They had nets over their cots but no glass in their windows. In the night Justa heard some crashing and banging in the "cottage" next to theirs when she appeared to be the only one awake. A young woman was in there alone. Luis, their native guide, explained the next morning that that was no problem. The monkeys just came in and inspected everything and knocked things around. Justa wanted toilet facilities in the middle of the night. There was no way of getting Jim's attention because he slept peacefully on his good ear. The only "latrine" was in a tent. The natives used the outdoors. Of course, she had no idea what she might run into in this little late night stroll. She took her kerosene lamp and found the tent without being threatened by any wild creatures although she did hear many strange sounds. She didn't linger long but returned quickly to their "cottage".

The group had good tours through the Rain Forest with Guide Luis using a scythe to cut the paths. He explained the different varieties and told how scientists study many trees, bushes, and plants that are or could be used in medications. Luis would often stop and hand them a particular little seed, leaf, frog or bug. But then after all, it was a rainforest, and it did rain. One day Luis cut a huge "leaf" from a tree and handed it Justa for an umbrella. Sometimes it was very slippery and not on level ground. Jim and a lady named Kay were teased about who won for having the most falls. Their backsides were covered with mud, but there were simple but satisfactory showers available when they returned to the lodge.

They were 120 feet above ground when they crossed on South America's first canopy walkway. It appeared to be swinging, and they felt very adventurous and yet thrilled to have this opportunity to be walking way up there above the treetops among wildlife that most people will never see. The foliage was so dense and luxurious and full of unusual creatures and different sounds.

TOO MUCH ADVENTURE? COULD THEY GET LOST OUT THERE?

Some days they had early morning bird watching. Another day they had a motor cruise to an area that bragged of having the largest water lilies in the world. Tourists had read about them in magazines. To get there they had to motor through water plants that sometimes caught their propellers. The engine died, and they wondered what they would do if they could not get it restarted. How would they ever get out of this mess of water plants? They were miles from nowhere. They were in water that no doubt had many snakes and other creatures in it. That would make a dirty swim pool look sparkling. They might be stranded in this desolate spot where no one could find them. But the boatman was finally able to get the props untangled and to restart the engine.

He maneuvered the small boat through and around lots of growth, and then there they were—those magnificent huge water lilies. Was it worth the trouble? Yes.

One day they visited the Yagua Indian Village. They shook hands with the chief in his grass skirt and listened to their history. The females were topless and were in red grass skirts and were usually pregnant. They did a lot of creative work with the natural products around them. When tourists came, they liked to make trades. One woman wanted Justa's blouse. Justa knew that she would and so brought an extra with her. Then she had a choice of one of the woman's creations. What she chose was a necklace that has the head of a caiman hanging on the string of beads made of jungle nuts or pits. The mouth opens up, and the teeth are still there. It looks like its relative, the alligator. When the woman then asked for Justa's shoes, Justa gave them to her and received back a necklace with a vicious piranha jaw to take home to Laurie. Justa had fun with her caiman head but never saw Laurie display her necklace.

Amazon female wants Justa's blouse

This whole trip was fascinating, and they were thrilled to have been a part of it. Fortunately they were all of a breed who could handle misadventure as well as adventure. The last day they had to get back to Iquitos to get a flight home. They had time to tour the town, although it was very poor compared to their homes. Elaine was walking alone and had her purse stolen. Justa and Jim didn't know that at the time. They were walking along the street with Bruce, who had his doctorate in marine biology and was assisting the tour director. There was another couple with them. Justa heard good dance music coming from one of the buildings. Bruce excused himself for a minute, and he ran up some stairs. He returned promptly and said, "*They're having a party and invited us to join them.*" Now, they were talking. Where there was danceable music, Justa couldn't hold still. Of course, she was all for going to the party. Jim was against it, but of course, he couldn't win this one. They joined these hospitable local people. Justa had a chance to display her bad Spanish, but nobody could compete with her on the dance floor. When Jim wasn't eager to dance, Bruce and Justa did; so then Jim did too. They enjoyed it, and their hosts were delighted. There are people of all kinds everywhere.

Dancing with Bruce in Iquitos

NOT YOUR NORMAL FUN TIME AT THIS AIRPORT

There was a bus to take them to the airport. This turned out to be a nightmare. There were so many people. They didn't have enough seats at the terminal. The plane didn't come, and didn't come, and didn't come. Everyone was exhausted. Some asked to be taken back to a hotel. However, there was only this one plane out until the next week, and they certainly didn't want to spend it there. A man and woman were standing next to each other with their carry-on between their feet. A good-looking Spanish-speaking woman came up to the lady and asked for help about something. This kind tourist tried to understand her and help her, but she really couldn't tell what was being said, and the woman left quickly. That's when the couple realized that the carry-on that held all their valuables, except fortunately her passport, were gone with the woman. A stranger pointed to another man and said that he was the thief. When police questioned this one, he had none of their possessions. That meant that there were two and maybe three culprits in the trick. The third one being the man who said that he saw the event. Perhaps he was the actual thief. It's even possible that the police were involved. Then there was the question of why a bag was checked through to Miami, and no one would claim it. Airline "officials" said that they couldn't take it because they didn't know what was in it. Perhaps thieves switched tags and will have someone else's valuable possessions. It was after midnight when their plane finally came, but it couldn't land because all the lights went out at the airport. That had to be resolved. And the trip home was just beginning! Justa has enough stories for a lifetime, but perhaps you have had enough of all this.

DID THE UNEXPECTED INHERITANCE CHANGE HER FROM A TRAVELLER TO A FARMER OR A JUNK DEALER?

Her father died in November 1971, her father-in-law in February 1972, and her Aunt Mabel in March 1972. It was a complete surprise when she and her brother inherited property from their Aunt Mabel. This was the girl who was adopted so her father would have a sister again.

She had left the big house in town, investments, and farm built in 1835, with nine outbuildings filled with old stuff. Their aunt thought she was poor, lived frugally and seldom got rid of anything. The attorney was the best around, but he was old too and was in the hospital. His secretary took his part in settling the Illinois estate. Justa's brother, Wes, lived in Rochester, New York and was involved with his job at Eastman Kodak. Justa had had practically no experience on a farm. When she was little, her family visited her father's biological brother on the pig farm in Michigan. At that time although they had a wonderful visit, she kept asking her mother when they would go home where she could get some real milk, the cold kind that came out of bottles—not the warm stuff out of cows of all things!

Justa and Jim lived in Danville, Illinois. It wasn't close, but it was closer; so she worked with the bank executor and made the decisions. Justa talked Jim into a week to vacation at Pheasant Run, a resort, on route 64 near the farm at Lily Lake. She said they could look over things during the day, then clean up and swim and have dinner and go to the theater in the evening. They had wall to wall items. She sorted and gave him the job of going through the old clothes and paper items. Not realizing the value of either, he kept a fire going and burned and burned. She found a stock certificate in the wastebasket. The two had quite an education and a lot of work. Her aunt had been in the nursing home, and others had been in her home ostensibly to work. Some cleaned up by helping themselves. Justa and Jim rearranged the furniture and realized how charming it really was.

Justa gave regular reports to her brother. She was dealing with the bank and the architect and the farmer on details. She hired the architect to get the farmhouse back to original style including chimneys at both ends, wooden floors beautifully refinished etc. They turned part of the pantry off the kitchen into a laundry room. One time she took her elderly mother up to the farm for several days so she could see the developments. There was no phone, and late one night when they were in bed, a car drove into the farmyard and stayed for awhile. Of course, the intruders didn't know that Justa and her Mom were in there basically defenseless. It was a little frightening, because they had no way to protect themselves if anyone was there to cause a problem.

BIG SALE BROUGHT BUYERS FROM EVERYWHERE

They eventually had a huge farm contents sale. Of course, she had hired a good auctioneer, but Justa was in on all the planning and work. She remembers the woman who said, "*You won't believe what I'm going to get for this brass bed in California*." When it started to sprinkle, everything in the farmyard had to be covered. One of the male customers came running up to Justa, "*What happened to my pictures?*" He had his eyes on certain treasures and did not want them to be missing. Although he hadn't bought them yet, in his mind they were his. There were many unusual antiques. Justa explained that things had been covered temporarily, and the sale would go on in minutes.

The bank executor had hired a man to check daily the big house on the Fox River in the town of Elgin. Workmen were making it into small apartments. Someone turned off the radiators in the house. By then it was winter and cold, and the radiators froze and broke and water poured all over everything and ruined all the improvements that the carpenters had made. No one took responsibility for having turned off the radiators. It was going to be too much of a pain to fix up that mess; so Justa who was after all first a wife, a mother, a daughter, a homemaker, and a volunteer, was disheartened but overworked said, "*Just sell it*." It was a big loss, but she was tired and decided to put her energies into the farm. Originally she had visualized turning that into something like Knott's Berry Farm in California.

GREAT CONFLAGRATION SADDENED JUSTA FARMER

Then there was the day the farm manager from the bank called to say there'd been a fire. He did not want her to come up to the farm. Everything had looked so nice after the restoration. He promised but didn't send the newspaper accounts. The tenant's son and a friend were smoking in that wonderful big barn with the hand-hewn timbers and had started the fire. It was quite a conflagration, and volunteer fire departments from all over the area were called. The man who had sold Justa the insurance got into the act and had all the water turned onto the farmhouse with the new shake shingles and all the reconstruction. The firemen used water from Lily Lake. It was across the road from the house but actually on their property. The trees around the lake burned, but of the nine "outbuildings" all that was left were the stable, machinery storage buildings, and the garage. The charm of the little milk house and other old buildings was gone. There was a lot of work to be done. Justa's dreams for a new Knott's Berry farm were gone. But they had restored what they could. They took down the windmill. Later she was sorry because it gave the place some charm. She has the State of Illinois Department of Agriculture Centennial Farm Certificate framed and hanging on the den wall with all the other family history.

Farm house saved from fire

Horses at farm

Justa on combine

Farm neighbor and his corn dryer

Farm manager showing Jim the tall corn

EXCELLENT NEW FARM MANAGER

After that, they had a very conscientious young man who did a good job of managing the farm and who was very helpful in explaining everything to Justa and Jim on each visit to the farm. She learned more. They repaired what they could of buildings and the fences. Until then the trustees were a big disappointment. Her brother missed all of this because of his distance away, but Justa kept him informed. She learned about raising corn and soy beans and could even climb up onto the combine and feel like a real farmer. She knew so little; so she went back to college and studied agricultural economics, agricultural mechanics, and antiques. The Danville Commercial News sent out a reporter to interview her. He wrote a flattering article saying how the students enjoyed having Justa in the class. She was pleasant, fun, knowledgeable, and her life experiences added to the success of the classes. The property was divided up into several parcels that were sold at different times. She learned quite a bit about real estate during those procedures. The last she heard was that that area is all built up with expensive homes.

STUDYING, BUYING, SELLING, WRITING ANTIQUES

Justa and Jim never sued anybody, not the firm doing the work on her Aunt Mabel's Elgin house, not the banker or executor, not the tenant whose son caused the big fire at the farm that destroyed all those buildings, and not the doctors who made mistakes in their surgeries. They just accepted the bad things along with the good things that came into their lives. They were unusual and perhaps foolish in that respect. Then they started going to estate sales, and Justa wrote about them for the Tri-State Trader. She was buying and collecting more dolls, antique hatpins, antique tumblers, berry bowls, thimbles etc. Jim didn't like going to the sales at first, but he went to please her just as she sat through so many football games to please him. He began to like the sales after he had his own collections including coins and toy banks. They had so much fun but had too much stuff. She'd clean up and dress the dolls and clean and repair anything they bought. This was therapy for her.

They had to have garage sales. Their sales were very popular because there were many interesting antique items. The sales were in a lovely neighborhood. People lined up way ahead of sale time.

One time at another sale she bought a violin that was still in the case. She took it out, looked at it and then put it back in. There was beautiful inlaid work on that instrument. Inside it said "Stradivarius". That auctioneer hadn't even taken it out for anyone to know that. Justa had played the viola, and she tried several bows on this. It didn't sound very good, but it probably wasn't the fault of the violin. She took it to several dealers. They convinced her that the Japanese had made instruments and printed that inside. She kept it on display by her baby grand piano. It was impressive. She eventually sold it at a profit, but of course nothing as much the amount it would be if this were genuine. Sometimes she wonders if she'd been taken on this too, and the dealers just wanted a steal.

One day on the way home from lunch at the Danville Country Club, she noticed a sale at a lovely big house in a good neighborhood. She convinced Jim to stop. They went in, and she asked the dealer about the pile of items out by the garage. He said that anything anyone wanted from there was free. Of course, she had to look. She immediately started tugging on what looked like an Oriental rug under the pile. Jim dressed for golf at the club and not the least interested in this junk, was embarrassed, but he wouldn't let her tug alone. It turned out to be a nice big quality antique Oriental rug in good condition. They managed with some help to get it folded and rolled up and into the trunk of the Cadillac. At home Justa insisted on sweeping the big garage, spreading out the rug and vacuuming it. She was amazed at how lovely it looked. She was furnishing an apartment for their son with antiques from her mother and other items that she had picked up. It was perfect.

At a club party that week an antique dealer knowledgeable on Oriental rugs started to tell her about the beautiful Oriental rug she had seen that weekend, but it got away from her because she didn't have any help. This lady had seen the same rug, gone home to get her big son to help, and by the time they returned it was gone. Justa smiled. She had a winner. She decided that she was now a glorified junk dealer. Justa Junk Dealer?

AFRICAN SAFARI AND DANCING AND SWAHILI 1977

Jim was the pastor parish chairman at the St. James United Methodist Church, and Justa always helped there. She had the key to the parsonage. They were friends with the pastor and his wife who suggested in 1977 that Jim and Justa must get away for a rest. They took a memorable trip the length of Africa with two other wonderful, congenial couples, Pinkie and Chris Christensen and Mim and Claire Riessen. She calls the Christensens the "host and hostess with the mostest". They entertain everyone so famously. Mim and Claire are the tennis playing Riessen family.

When they were on safari in Kenya, they had a guide whose native tongue was Swahili. Justa asked if she could sit in the van with him and learn some of his language. He liked the idea. She learned a few phrases. That evening at a gathering of the tourists, she told of that experience. A young Frenchman asked her to teach him what she learned. She had a book that had three columns giving the English, French and Swahili phrases. She could use it to translate from one to either of the others quite easily. It was great fun. For example: Where is the lavatory please? In French that is: Ou est le lawabo, s'il vous plait? In Swahili that is Maalani ni wapi? For Justa languages are fun. For the others it was just entertainment watching her with the Frenchman.

Another day on safari with a different driver-guide, the van broke down. This driver did not stay within range of the others as they were instructed to do. He had been conceited and thought he didn't have to. They were supposed to be available if another needed help. They had no assistance. This was before the days of cell phones. The driver was out in that hot sun with the raised hood and his head over the hot engine. Theoretically they were in wild animal land, but none were visible at the time. They hoped he knew what he was doing. Usually the tourists just stayed in the van and poked their heads out the opening in the top to take their pictures. Of course, Justa got out and was walking around when she heard some music seeming to come from the wilderness beyond. Then a native appeared out of nowhere carrying a battery-operated radio. It was broadcasting danceable music. The next thing her companions saw was Justa linking arms with the native and dancing up a storm. This wasn't too far from where they had seen elephants, zebras, giraffes and lions. They could see Kilamanjaro off in the distance. It's in Tanzania. Then they heard the sputtering engine settle down, and then back to their housing for the night.

Justa dancing with native when on Safari

Jim dancing with belly dancer

At some point on that African trip somewhere around pyramids and the Sphinx and desert, a belly dancer appeared, grabbed hold of Jim, rolled up his pant legs and was belly-dancing with him. There was a big smile on his face, and there were grins on the faces of his companions. It was like the time in Nome, Alaska that Justa was pulled from the audience, had a boa thrown around her neck, and she was part of the show. Justa is a natural ham, and for her that was no problem. But this time it was the shy Jim and his new acquaintance who were the stars. And everyone loved it, because for him it was so out of character.

SEATS ALL TAKEN FLIGHT CLOSED

In order to visit Luxor from Cairo, it was necessary to arise early and be ready to be at the airport at 4:30 a.m. When they arrived, the tour director, John, told them just to sit down there, and he would take care of the arrangements. When he spoke to the ticket agent, he was told that there were no more seats, and therefore the flight was closed. Suddenly John grew about ten feet tall, banged his fist on the counter and shouted for all to hear: "Then, by God, open it." Suddenly a door opened, and a string of tired, little people, came out. John signaled his group to come, and they walked right onto the plane and into their seats. That certainly shows the advantage of touring with a big powerful company that has all the business contacts.

The story of their visit there is a book in itself. There they saw Angela Lansbury for the first time and some of the filming of "Death on the Nile". Then they enjoyed her television performances many times. When it was time for the return flight, John warned his group that there was no reserved seating. When the plane was announced, they were to run as fast as they could out onto the tarmac and grab a seat or goodness knew when they would ever get back to Cairo, let alone home. Justa and Pinkie weren't shy and took him literally. They put aside any courtesy, fairness, or ladylike training their mothers had instilled in them and started running. They were the first to get to the plane, and up the steps. Pinkie, who is a football fan, shouted to her friend, "You made the best end around run I've ever seen". Then she quickly threw jackets and hats on seats in the NO SMOKING SECTION to save them for husbands and friends. There was still some smoking allowed on most planes.

ETHIOPIA: GREEK AMBASSADOR AND CLERIC

Near the end of the African trip their plane stopped briefly in Addis Ababa, Ethiopia. Justa bought an unusual bracelet filigreed and with elephant's hair braiding that always draws attention. On the continuing flight Justa suggested that she and Jim sit separately so they'd meet others. A Greek Orthodox cleric chose to sit with Justa. Her seatmate with his big beard and in his religious garb was a sight to behold. He was fascinated with Justa and couldn't stop talking to her and educating her on the origin of her name and everything Greek and religious. Emperor Haile Selassie was his friend and had given him a palace and all the help it needed. Of course, in his mind the emperor was wonderful. It was a little troubling that he sat with his face too close to hers, but the experience was worth it. He volunteered to be their guide the next day in Athens. Justa is often a better talker than listener and always expects equal time! He liked her and talked constantly and thoroughly enjoyed himself. He was the top cleric in Ethiopia and accustomed to holding the floor. Outtalking Justa is an accomplishment in itself, but it was interesting to her.

The Greek Ambassador to Ethiopia chose to sit with Jim across the aisle and down a couple of rows. As the cleric had nothing but good things to say about the emperor, across the way and talking to Jim was the ambassador railing against Haile Selassie. He had an entirely different opinion of the man. He spoke of how awful he was and all the terrible things he had done. It was quite an education for the couple who compared notes later. The emperor was deposed in 1975.

CRUISE ON THE BAY OF BENGAL STOP AT PHUKET ISLAND, THAILAND

On a Bay of Bengal cruise they stopped at Phuket Island, Thailand. There was a division of interest for the sexes. As they walked along the water there were magnets drawing the men's eyes to the gorgeous seaside that was enhanced by the sight of the nude bathers. As for the ladies they were interested in climbing up the hillside to a settlement renowned for the lovely needlework created by the natives there. The blouses were just elegant with decorative embroidered designs, often white on white. Bear with me if I jump around the world a bit. Justa's head is full of so much stuff that she wants me to tell you, so I'm trying to get the most interesting out to you in readable form. She's not as sharp a cookie as she once was. You probably already guessed that part.

1992 TOUR ISRAEL WITH ARAB MUSLIM GUIDE AND CHRISTIAN MINISTER TRIP ORGANIZER

After a lifetime of living in a Christian home and hearing over and over again the Bible stories, they visited the Holy Land. They saw the Dome of the Rock, which is a holy shrine for Muslims, Christians, and Jews. That is where Abraham is said to have offered his son Isaac for sacrifice. They had entertained in their home foreign students whom they treated as their own children. One was a Muslim from Iraq. They had entertained United Nations delegates who were Muslims. Justa had never really thought of them in any way but as other human beings, never the enemy.

Their leaders on this trip were superb and showed them every place they had ever heard of. Three tourists were shot the day before their arrival in Israel, and they walked right through that area. Police were protecting the old city where the killings happened. There were soldiers everywhere, and yet they didn't really feel afraid. One soldier was petting a dog. They climbed up on the Mount of Olives and saw ancient olive trees and an antique olive press. She shared a donkey ride with an Arab coming back down. She bought a beautiful hand embroidered caftan in Bethany right across the path from Lazarus' tomb. They saw ostriches raised at a Kibbutz, the Wall of Jericho, and the Masada that Herod built to feel safe from the Jews. She waded in the Mediterranean and the Dead Seas and had a boat ride on the Sea of Galilee. They saw people baptized in the dirty Jordan River. They visited the Church of Annunciation where the angel is said to have told Mary about the baby. In Bethlehem they visited the Church of the Nativity which was built over the place of Jesus' birth. They also saw the holy manger. They visited the Holocaust Museum and the Wailing Wall in Jerusalem. They walked on the Via Dolorosa where Jesus walked carrying the cross.

This trip made the Bible stories easier to visualize. However, once again Justa could not help but feel so sad that religion, instead of bringing love and peace, has caused so much hatred and bloodshed. In her mind she pictures a planet where all persons would aim to live in a way that would make life better not only for themselves and but also everyone else. Throughout history people have tried to figure out what life is all about, where it began, and where it will end, instead of living each day the best that they can.

THEY VISIT 100 YEARS LATER THE PLANTATION WHERE HER DAD FOUND HIS SISTER

Justa's father was adopted when he was two years of age. His biological father was no more, and his mother was young and unable to care for the children. There was a sister, Mamie, about five years of age who had helped to take care of him. He missed her terribly. The mother was surely busy with the baby brother, Arney. In school when Justa was assigned the task of writing her family history, she wrote this story: A Free Methodist minister and his wife in Elgin, Illinois adopted John, her father. His sister, Mamie, with a nametag around her neck was sent alone by train from Illinois to Mississippi to live with a retired doctor-plantation-owner (born in 1822), and his young wife, his third. The baby Arney went to live with a blind pig farmer and his wife in Michigan. The teacher wrote on Justa's paper, *"You're a very good writer with a terrific imagination, but this was supposed to be a true story."* It **was** the truth, as she knew it. The children missed each other terribly. John's parents adopted a little girl, Mabel, so that he would have a sister. However, he could not get Mamie out of his mind. They tried so hard to find each other. John's adoptive parents were helpful. When John and Mamie located each other, they tried to find Arney. In his case, he could read, but his parents couldn't. When the agency sent word that the two older children wanted to find him, he was the one who read the letter. He wasn't sure how to tell his parents. He didn't want to hurt them, but he did want to see his biological family if possible.

The family is one of nature's masterpieces.

—George Santayana

In 1905 at age 17 John finally located Mamie. He had finished high school, and business school, and had a job. They wrote loving letters to each other and then to their younger brother Arney and even located and had visits with their birth mother. That would be Justa's biological grandmother. She had remarried a fine man and helped raise his children, and then he helped her find hers. Justa and Jim actually went to visit her in California for the first time near the end of World War 2 when Jim was temporarily stationed there.

It was 1908 before John could visit Mamie at the Dupree Plantation near Raymond (near Jackson), Mississippi. They romped and played like little children. At that time the plantation was over 1,000 acres. John was talented with the camera and took wonderful pictures. They kept in close touch for the rest of their lives. When Justa last visited her Aunt Mamie, the elderly lady, kept offering her things. Justa would not take anything. She insisted her aunt keep the little she had herself. Finally Justa said,

"There is something that I would appreciate, the letters that you and Dad wrote when you first found each other."

That pleased her Aunt Mamie. After her death, those letters and also some interesting other papers and letters from the aged doctor were sent to Justa. Some of these are of great historical interest.

Dr. Dupree (age 86) works with Allen

Antique picture of Dupree House

John on his first visit there 1908

Mamie on two sides of the gate.

JUSTA WAS ASKED FOR HELP TO PUT DUPREE HOUSE ON NATIONAL REGISTER

About 1980 Justa received a phone call from a stranger saying that a young couple, Brenda and Richard Dunlap had purchased the Dupree property and wanted to get it on the National Register of Historic Homes. They were told that Justa was the one who could give them the information they needed to do that. She sent them most of the papers and the few little personal items that belonged there. The couple was very appreciative and was able to accomplish the feat. They sent her a copy of the certificate showing the Dupree property registered. They invited Justa and Jim to stop to meet them on their trip from Illinois to or from Florida. They did visit and saw that the home was full of lovely antiques and history. It was very nice, but the couple had work to do outside. They had a much smaller acreage than at the time of John's visit.

After Brenda and Richard purchased the Dupree House, Richard became ill and passed on. Justa and Jim had their hands full with business and family responsibilities, and they lost touch with the young folks when they moved to Florida in 1984. She often wondered how they were doing. In 2005 Justa was trying to finish writing this book that she had worked on for several years. That place and Aunt Mamie had been such an important part of her father's life. She really wanted to include that story. She had tried to contact three sources that should have been able to help her, but they did not respond. One was the director of the Archives whose signature was on the certificate, the church, and the post office. The fault was partly because Brenda had remarried and her name was changed and possibly because Justa did not have full enough addresses and so no one actually received the letters.

Brenda had lived alone on the plantation for about 15 years. Of course, Justa didn't know anything about this. However, she was now more determined than ever to find her. Finally one day out of the blue she called Laurie and said, "I just can't get Aunt Mamie, the Dupree Plantation, and those kids out of my mind." In less than two minutes Laurie called back and said, "Turn on your computer, Mom. Type in Dupree. You'll see that and Mamie's Cottage." She did that and found phone numbers and email address for the Dupree House and Mamie's Cottage. She knew then that that was the correct place. They must have moved Aunt Mamie's little house from Raymond to the plantation and turned it into a bed and breakfast business. She called Brenda. Later her new husband, Charles Davis, said that she had cried and said, *"I thought that I had lost her."* The two ladies were both very excited. They planned for Justa and Jim to visit and stay in Aunt Mamie's Cottage.

RETURN TO PLANTATION STAY IN AUNT MAMIE'S COTTAGE

Brenda, Charles, Jim with historical papers

Charles, Brenda, and Justa

In July 2005 it was 100 years since Justa's Dad located Mamie, his biological sister, at the Dupree Plantation in Mississippi. Now Justa and Jim had a wonderful time as guests in Mamie's Cottage where they had last visited with her. Justa had a few more items to give Brenda. Charles said later that Brenda cried, "*I thought I had lost her.*" Brenda Davis from the Dupree Plantation gave Justa "ego boost two" when she said, "I've often wondered where I would be if I had never met you"

Justa was so pleased to spend time with Brenda and Charles. She's been an outstanding tour guide of her fascinating home. She says much of that is because of all the wonderful stories she has been able to tell of its history and Mamie. The two couples learned from each other.

There were old letters of Dr. Dupree's. Justa could not see well enough to read and understand them. She suggested that Charles read out loud what he thought the words were, and she would sit at the computer to write and print it. Well, it was amazing because their families had lived there for a long time and recognized the names mentioned in the Civil War letters. Their descendents lived not far away. This was printed so that all guests could read it without hurting the original. They considered one letter museum quality. They have this wonderful bed and breakfast, and guests are shown through the old plantation big house. Brenda has a reputation for being the outstanding tour guide of the homes in the area on the National Register of Historic Homes. Her stories of Mamie are the most appreciated.

Brenda put an invitation in the newspaper inviting anyone who had known "Miss Mamie" to come to a party at the Dupree House to meet her niece. There was a nice group of people who had stories to tell of their relationship with her. One of the younger men who came, gave Justa a hug and said, "*We are relatives, you know, because she was my housemother.*" She was loved throughout the area for the good things she did for young people. The trauma she must have felt when she had to leave her mother and travel alone that long distance to find a new mother made her especially suited to help the young. The story is that as a five-year-old she traveled with an ID tag about her neck as she rode alone from Chicago to Mississippi. She grew into a very special lady.

Dr. Dupree owned the cotton plantation that was reputed to have been the largest in the area at that time. He was a Civil War veteran born in 1822 and married to Patty, his third wife, a young woman who very much wanted a daughter. Mamie was the one very kind and loving person who read to the old gentleman when his sight was almost gone. Mamie called Patty "Aunty" instead of mother because she knew her birth mother, but they loved each other dearly and lived together for years after everyone else was gone. Justa helped Brenda and Charles, but they also helped her learn some of her aunt's history.

I have recently heard that Mississippi State Representative Mary Ann Stevens was concerned about remodeling Mississippi historic buildings without the proper knowledge. She broached the idea of having a position to handle that. On February 2, 2006 Brenda started working as an architectural historian at the state capitol in Jackson. She was the perfect choice for the job. She has such a fine background and understands the archives and history and so will be a real asset in making decisions in changing any of the old buildings. This means that she will have fewer tours of her home.

JUSTA MUST TALK

Eighty years ago in grade school Justa and her friend, Carna, had to stay after school and write ten times "*I must not talk*". Well, she thinks that she must talk. Their lives have been enhanced by this ability to communicate with anyone anywhere. She's glad that she could say to her young husband, "*Let's go to Europe*". He didn't think he could leave work for that long." She said, "*I think you could*!" That was the beginning of their wonderful, extensive worldwide travels. Jim always knows what she thinks about something. She **tells him**.

On a long airline flight she found herself in the middle seat with a very large, stern-looking man in what was usually **her aisle seat.** Her carry-on was under the seat in front of her with those essential glaucoma drops in it. The man looked unapproachable, but she turned to him and said, "*Sir, I have a problem.*" He jumped up immediately, and pleasantly said, "*Oh, yes, Ma'am.*" She explained her situation. Problem solved! Then she felt like a little girl as she looked up at this big man and said,

"Sir, would you mind if I put my head on your shoulder? I need to get my head back to get my drops in." He gave her a big grin as he replied, *"Not at all."*

They learned that they were to be on the same Mediterranean cruise. He was a bright man with a lovely wife whom they enjoyed for the whole cruise. They just had to talk. She has always made an effort to learn some of the language in any country they visited. Her accent was not good, but she was skillful with pantomime. That effort helped in communicating with the natives and really got their interest. In college her professors didn't tell her not to talk. Students were just told that they had to eat dinner at a table of their choosing, but they would have to speak only the language at that table if they wanted to eat. She chose the French. That turned out to be a good choice through the years.

1978 KWEILIN (GUILIN), CHINA

In Kweilin, China 1978 as Justa and Jim walked along the street she spoke to the first person they met by putting her hands together as in prayer, bowing slightly and saying "*knee how*". This was a typical young woman with long black pigtails and wearing a Mao shirt. They weren't accustomed to blondes. But she grinned and bowed and "knee howed" back. With some Mandarin but mostly demonstrating, Justa asked where she might find those little black flat heeled one strap "Mary Jane type" canvas shoes the young ladies were wearing. The girl indicated she'd guide them there. Suddenly people seemed to come out of the woodwork.

She "knee howed" them and pointed at Justa with a grin and told them what was going on. The growing crowd would bow to them and "knee how". She felt like the Pied Piper of Hamelin as they reached the old-fashioned department store with their entourage.

There were wide wooden stairs leading up to a big almost bare room with accoutrements similar to what was available in her childhood. Their new friend pointed to the long wooden bench where they were to sit as she explained to the clerk. The whole group lined up behind the couple as she was fitted in her new shoes. Grins were everywhere as Justa nodded that that was what she wanted. Then there was applause for the successful adventure. The whole entourage walked with them back to their hotel grinning and babbling a few lines that she really understood. They bowed and waved goodbye as Justa and Jim entered their hotel.

Justa's glad that the wonderful first grade teacher who taught her so much failed in the effort to stop her from talking. If she couldn't talk, she wouldn't be able to communicate with all the wonderful, talented people who have added a new dimension to their lives, and broadened their horizons. When her husband talks about her, he says, "*Phyl-z doesn't know a stranger.*" She takes that as a compliment. What he means is that she is comfortable talking with the CEO, any employee, any color, any tongue. She admits that she talks to the animals too. She whistles as she walks along where the birds nest. She assumes that those Mockingbirds are singing back. She says, *"All I can say is that it works for me, and I'm one happy lady. Some people choose to be happy, and some don't. I do."*

The grand essentials of happiness are: something to do, something to love, and something to hope for.

—Allan K. Chalmers

PROMISE HOUSE 1978

In 1978 Justa was aware of the mental health facilities being closed down and the need for day care locally. When she heard about Promise House, the new day care treatment center that was being started in Danville, Illinois, she wanted to help. All they had was the house and of course, the people. Her mother had died the previous year. Her possessions were good and some still available. She knew that mother would be pleased to have them used at Promise House. She visited and talked to the "coordinator", Harry Barnhart. She took some pictures that had hung on her mother's walls and put those up. She saw that they needed window treatments. She took all of the extra curtains and draperies she could find and took those to Promise House. She also took her portable sewing machine, ironing board and iron. She also bought two pairs of draperies at the Salvation Army. With this supply and a little work, she was able to take care of all of the windows.

Mr. Barnhart and his assistants were counseling the troubled individuals who came there daily. They were able to get jobs for some. Justa realized that they could use other clothing. She told her friends what she thought was needed, and they were eager to help. The donated clothing was put into a room that Justa dubbed THE CLOSET. It was free to anyone who could use it. The next step was to create a library. Mr. Barnhart made a room available for that, and friends offered books. Bingo. They had a library that grew as others contributed.

Justa had moved to Florida and hadn't thought about this for years until she found a beautiful thank you letter that she had received in 1978 and had never thrown away. Promise House was such a valuable asset for Danville. She hopes that it continued to grow and serve the afflicted. Finding that letter with a pile of others reminded her. It's important to compliment and thank others at every opportunity. It's easy and means so much to the recipient.

I can no other answer make but thanks, and thanks, and ever thanks.

Twelfth Night, William Shakespeare

ILLINOIS TO FLORIDA

Justa and Jim had vacationed in Florida since the early fifties. They knew the area well. In 1983 when they were packing their car from their stay on Longboat Key, the car really slanted to the rear. It was so overloaded. There had been a big storm, and Justa had picked up a wonderful assortment of large unusual shells to have packages for all of the children of the neighborhood. She just had too many hobbies. Their backs were tired. Justa said, "*Why are we doing this? I can't get my baby grand piano in the trunk, and I really miss my other toys. Why don't we just have one home? We could live and travel from here.*" Jim responded, *"It's all right with me.*

They found a great lot for their condo on Sarasota Bay, chose a floor plan, and signed the papers. They had the cash. The real estate broker was ecstatic. When they arrived back at their rental property, there was a message, "*That property was just sold ahead of you. We can find another.*" The next morning on their way back to this realtor, Justa said, *"Why don't we check at Wildewood Springs on the way past? It was such a nicely landscaped place.*" They had rented there at one time. When they entered the office, the only person there was on the phone. They looked at the pictures of units and floor plans and were ready to leave. The young person said, *"Just a moment."* They responded, *"Thanks, but we really want something larger than we see here.*"

She got off the phone and inquired, *"Just what are you looking for? We have one unit F left at 2300 square feet. Are you interested?*" They were. This was in the new part of Wildewood Springs that was called Spring Lakes. They looked at the place. They saw that it was almost finished so they could visualize what the completed project would be. They smiled at each other and agreed that this was exactly what they had been looking for. They listed the additions that they wanted. They bought that condo in less time than it takes them to choose a cantaloupe. Justa made an appointment with a decorator at the popular Kanes Furniture

Store to choose wallpaper and paint colors and two Barcoloungers and some lanai furniture.

They turned the follow-up over to this young lady and headed north to Danville, Illinois to sell their home. That occurred almost immediately, but they had too much furniture and so many beautiful things. People began to say, "*If you can't take this with you, I'd love to buy it.*" Justa had had a lot of experience including the big farm sale. That was the 1835 farmhouse and nine outbuildings loaded with treasures. At that time Justa had gone to school to study antiques and then went to every moving or estate sale. It wasn't that profitable. It was just a hobby.

So now she decided to have a silent auction. It was just to be for friends and neighbors. It turned out that everybody was a friend or neighbor. Phone calls came, "*Justa, do you remember me? We knew you from PTA or Scouts when our children were young?*" "*I've told Susan about your sale. Do you remember her? She'd like to come.*" "*Would it be all right if I brought Don? He has a new house and could use a lot of things.*" Justa allowed one week with a noon deadline. When people came, they were given a number. Each item for sale had a paper by it where a person could sign their number and put in a bid. The next person passing could put his or her number and a higher bid. They asked questions about almost everything in the house. One doctor kept coming back about a picture in the dining room that Justa planned to take with her. He kept insisting and saying, "*Everything is for sale at a price. What will you take for it?*" She finally gave in because although it was special, she didn't really need it.

Everybody had a delightful time because there were so many treasures. Friends and neighbors kept returning. It was fun for all. When the deadline came that noon, there were still very nice items that they just couldn't take with them to Florida. She let the buyers bid and accepted the highest amount without any limits although everyone knew that they were worth more. Their friends were just happy to have something that had belonged to them. Justa and Jim still had plenty to ship south, but they knew exactly where they planned to put everything including hanging the pictures.

SUDDENLY THEY WERE FLORIDIANS

When they finally arrived at their Florida condo, they found that Kanes Furniture Co. had completed the decorating, but the new Barcoloungers had been delivered but not covered. When six ceiling fans were installed after the chair delivery, the unprotected new Barcoloungers were covered with dust! That was exasperating, but in general everything pleased them.

Their furniture came from the north, and everything quickly found its place. They were home. They loved to swim lengths of the pool and to sit in the spa and relax with new neighbors who always said, "*We think we've died and gone to heaven*." They asked each new acquaintance if he or she knew anyone who might tune their piano. They were told which neighbors had pianos. It turned out that these people also played bridge; so they organized a bridge group. They found other tennis players. Justa was asked to be social chairperson. She organized everything and started a "library". That was simply an area above the mailboxes where everyone could place the books and magazines that they no longer needed and take any they wanted. She took a tape player and tapes to the pool where they exercised. They soon knew almost everybody. Jim became treasurer and then president of their cluster.

JUSTA THE ORGANIZER TOOK OVER

They were chatting one evening with condo neighbors when Justa asked, *"Who is in charge of the pools?" "The roads?" "Security?" "The tennis courts?" "Water?" "Lights?"* They suddenly realized that the developers had created five separate associations without any connection or description on how things would be run. Two of the associations each owned a pool, but everyone was told they could use either. The tennis courts still belonged to the developer. Justa immediately invited the leaders of each association over to their lanai and said, *"This is to discuss common responsibilities and interests."* She called this the Spring Lakes Group, and they met regularly and took one problem at a time. Justa was the organizer, but there was a lawyer, an electrician, a jack of all trades, and two businessmen. They named her chairperson, and she ran it like a democracy. Every topic was discussed, and each person could give his opinion, and the majority ruled.

When the developer tried to sell other parcels for other uses, the group had petitions and went to the courthouse, and let their opinions be known. They often had different ideas, but they were always courteous and able to compromise. Whatever was best for the whole neighborhood usually won out. They always tried to be fair. They really liked each other. The developer, Neal and Neal, had sold to Amerifirst, and soon the bank was ready to turn over everything to the resident owners. The officials talked to Justa. She said, *"You will have to make the group a legal entity as written in the documents. The tennis courts will have to be resurfaced and given to us. There is some roadwork to be done. We expect you to pay the attorney fees."* That's the gist of it as I remember it. They were on the West Coast of Florida, and the bank's attorney, a female, lived on the East Coast. The ladies worked together very well. Everything was settled by phone calls or mail. The group attorney and all members approved and signed. Justa's address was listed as the official residence. When the bank's manager was ready to move out, he gave Justa all the oversize Spring Lakes envelopes, license plates, and everything left in his office concerning Spring Lakes. The group continued as the Spring Lakes Council of Associations and was now legal.

After Justa had taken this responsibility for seven years, two as chairperson of the group, and five as president of the council, she decided that that was enough. She wrote a letter stating that it was time for Jim and her to be relieved of all decision making for Spring Lakes. Her associates had a lovely party for her, a plaque and a letter that she treasures. She enjoyed helping, but it was hard work, and there were others who could take over.

THEY STILL HELPED THEY NEVER STOP

Justa and Jim still helped as they could with the condo association but in a simpler way. Jim was always expected to audit the books. Residents seemed to think they should just tell Justa their problems, and she'd take care of them. One day she was walking around with clippers in her hand. A lady came out and complained that the bushes by her entrance needed to be cut shorter. Justa said that all you have to do is take your little clippers and cut off about four inches. "*Well, I couldn't do that. I'm an old lady." "Oh, and how old would that be*?" questioned Justa. "*I'm 74*" was the reply. *"Oh, then let me do it. I'm 84*". It only took a couple minutes. Justa wrote an article on what it means to be in a condominium association. I wish she could find it or maybe she should rewrite it. Most people have no clue that the board members are neighbors who are unpaid volunteers working and making decisions for them. Unless there is on-grounds management, that's a big job for the condo board. Residents have an investment there and should all share in the responsibilities.

60TH WEDDING ANNIVERSARY

On their 60th anniversary Justa played golf with the ladies at the El Conquistador Country Club. She finished lunch except for the dessert and excused herself with, "*I shall return.*" When asked what the champagne flutes were for, she just smiled and shrugged her shoulders. Then she went to the manager's office that he had offered for a dressing room. Laurie was there with the 1941 wedding gown, veil, slippers and jewelry. Jim, dressed in tuxedo and patent leather shoes, greeted her with a big smile. Laurie quickly dressed her mother and then gave the signal to fellow golfer and beautiful pianist, Dorothy Whaley, who played the wedding march.

With heads held high and smiling faces, the bridal couple walked in amongst the tables and greeted their friends. Laurie handled the long train. The startled luncheon guests, golfers and bridge players alike, couldn't believe the transition from golf clothes to wedding gown in five minutes. Wine was served to all. There were comments, "beautiful", "amazing", and "*I wouldn't be able to get one foot in mine.*" There were hugs and toasts. Jim was most impressive when he grinned, held his glass high, and said, "*To the next ten*!" Then as quickly as that switch, she was now back into golf clothes and finishing dessert with fellow golfers. Jim and Laurie packed up the wedding clothes and were on their way home But there was more.

60th anniversary in 1941 gown

They took a 60th wedding anniversary cruise. When they participated in the newly-wed-not-so-newly-wed competition, the men were asked how was the sex on the first night of their honeymoon. Her husband quickly announced, "*Impossible*!" Honest, I guess. Of course, it brought laughs and they won a bottle of wine. Then the commentator came on the mike and said, "*There were mints on the table as you left the dining room, I have a bottle of wine for anyone who can bring me some mints.*"

Justa never had taken the mints before, but for some reason she had that night. She ran up to him with her supply. There was a second bottle of wine. A little later, the master of ceremonies said, "*Now, the first man who comes up with lipstick on his forehead will win a bottle of champagne.*" Justa grabbed her purse, took out the lipstick, swung it across Jim's forehead to make a red mark and said, "*Run, go, go.*" Of course, he won another bottle. Then there was an announcement that the ship's officers wanted to dance with the ladies. Justa looked up, and the captain was at her side asking her for a dance. He was good, but of course not as good as Jim. At the end when he offered her a bottle of wine, she smiled and said, "*Thank you, but no. It was my pleasure. I don't really drink. I will give these to the folks sitting around us here.*"

Good humor is one of the best articles of dress one can wear in society.

William Makepeace Thackeray

ONE BULL'S EYE AT A TIME

Justa told me about this email that she sent to a friend: "Dear Carol, I'm sorry that we didn't get to see you when we were in Washington, but when we realized that you had other family coming too, it wasn't going to work. We were just too far away. We had a great time with you and all the others at the ballet in Orlando, seeing Bethany perform, and the wonderful dinner party afterwards. That was probably fortunate that you and I couldn't get together on this trip. I learned something years ago that I thought of at this time.

We were invited to a big party at a ranch. When we arrived, we saw that the host had many activities planned. His first question to me was 'How good are you at archery?' I made some smart remark such as, 'excellent'. Actually I wasn't bad, but I shouldn't have answered that way. He handed me a bow and arrow. At quite a distance, I stood up, looked at the target and shot a bull's eye! Other guests were very impressed. Now the lesson is this. When you hit a bull's eye, curtsy, smile, or say thank you to the admirers. Go on to something else! You've hit the bull's eye. That's it. Needless to say my next efforts weren't even close. That's how it was at the Orlando Ballet gathering with you. I had wondered about you for so long. I was delighted to see you. We had such a nice visit together. That was a bull's eye. We didn't have to do it again so soon. We can try another time later. Hope all went well with your visitors."

HEALTH PROBLEMS

Justa had had cancer and several surgeries, but to handle the stress she played hard. She loved to dance and swim. She played tennis and golf and bridge. Then on December 17, 2002 she was serving at tennis and suddenly couldn't talk when she tried to say, "*I think I'd better stop.*" She couldn't breathe. She objected strongly with a shake of the head when friends wanted to call 911, but they had to do something. They called First Care. Technicians took one look at her and immediately had her in an ambulance. She was in that when she heard voices say that her blood pressure was 200 over something, and she was very pale and her lungs sounded funny. There was a question of survival. She spent most of the day in the emergency room. Her family stayed there.

In the late afternoon she was moved to a regular room. As they wheeled her in, she thought she saw a black person on the side, but she wasn't fully conscious yet. Then she realized there were two beds in this rather small room. A curtain almost touched her body, and there was a big form touching the curtain from the other side. She had to know; so in her sweetest voice she inquired, "*May I ask with whom I might be sharing this room?*" A very deep but pleasant voice responded, "*I'm Mary*". Justa introduced herself. There were questions and answers. They opened the curtain and faced each other with smiles.

Mary was happy to have a pleasant companion because the previous occupant of this bed had treated her like the maid. Justa was to take Coumadin to thin her blood. Mary had a booklet on the topic and gave it to her. Later that evening Justa thought, "*I can't lie around like this, my muscles will atrophy*". So she crawled out of bed. She was normally very active. She didn't realize that this current problem could be lethal. Immediately Mary cried out, "*Get back in bed. You're supposed to lie still.*" She was about to do her stretching exercises. Her new friend cried out, "*No, no, no*" and rang the bell for the nurse who immediately came in and put Justa back into bed. She spoke in a respectful manner, but what the message meant was, "*Are you out of your mind? Don't you realize the seriousness of this? You're to lie still. Don't get out of bed again.*"

Justa tried to behave, but she was always so active that it was hard for her to lie still. She was lucky to have this roommate at that time. Mary shared her problems, and Justa listened. She realized how lucky she was. The medication took hold, and she fell asleep. Justa's family and friends sent flowers and cards. When Laurie brought a special arrangement for Mary, Mary acted like that was the nicest thing that had ever happened to her. Then they moved Justa to a private room and Mary to a special section where she could get the therapy she needed. After numerous tests and specialists, the diagnosis was pulmonary embolism possibly caused by the cancer medication. The other possibility could be that it was caused from the foot and ankle clots sustained in a fall on the Queen Mary during a recent trip with the Seabee veterans. Her feet had turned purple from heel to toe. She hadn't been able to walk and had to use a wheel chair. But she had forgotten all that. She tends to forget the bad and just remembers the good. This time she stayed in the hospital one week but was allowed to return home for Christmas Eve with Coumadin to thin her blood.

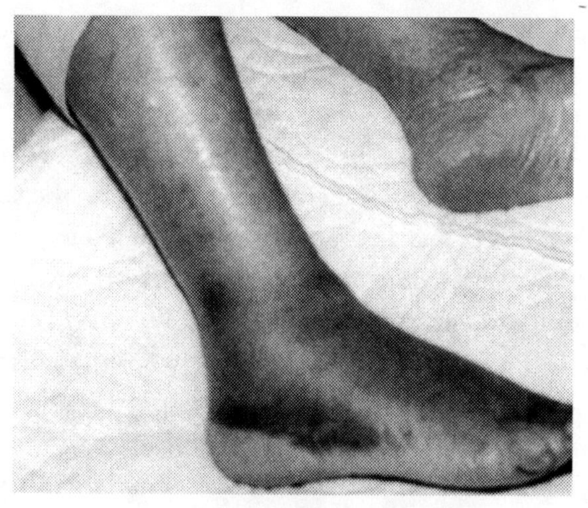

Sprained ankles from Queen Mary 1

HEADLINES TWO ELDERLY WOMEN MISSING 1998

These weren't just any two women. They were Jim's sisters and Justa's classmates. A call came from Marin County in California. Their niece, Debbie, had sent word that her 80-year-old mother, Louise, who lived in Greenbrae, and Aunt Doris, aged 78, had disappeared. Louise had picked up Doris in San Anselmo on Wednesday, and they were going to take a little ride. Then she would visit Debbie in Redwood City the next day, but she did not arrive. Debbie explained to Chris Marcuse, the Twin Cities Police detective in charge of the case, that this was frightening because her mother was a very responsible person. She was a national champion race walker. The detective did not immediately send up a helicopter because he didn't know where to look. He was told about Louise's power walking and many of the trails that she hiked. There were four or five towns they might have visited.

Debbie immediately made fliers and put them up on posts all over the area. She knew that it was a major problem. The police telephoned the television stations and notified anybody who could possibly help. They searched for the car in the areas where Debbie thought they might have parked and walked. Justa and Jim and other family members were on the East Coast, distressed and didn't know how to help. Finally a woman called in that there was a red, two-door Ford Festive parked near one of these areas, and it had been there for several days. Now they knew where to look. There were more headlines.

Barbie, Glenn, Louise, Jim, Doris
(Louise and Doris were missing)

WOMAN FOUND ALIVE - SISTER STILL MISSING

The family was relieved that Doris was found but worried more about Louise. Doris was found sunburned, dehydrated, and disoriented in a shallow creek in that remote, rugged Marinwood Canyon. The temperature got up to 102 F on Saturday. According to the search coordinator, Bob Thompson of the Sheriff's Department, the ladies were seen walking near Valleystone Drive about 2:30 p.m. Wednesday, the day that they started.

Searchers filled that area after a resident reported at noon Friday about the red car. Louise had walked this trail before, but rains had washed much of it away. When the sisters started the walk, it was level ground, but it changed into a steep rocky deer path that crosses a winding creek. Doris was found about a mile and a half from their starting point and ten feet off the path. There was speculation that Doris slipped in the loose gravel and fell and that Louise tried to help her and slid down into the canyon bottom too. Then she may have told her sister to stay by the water and she would go for help. Then she too may have been lost. Exertion in that heat may have contributed to disorientation. The wonderful searchers were from the Marin County Search and Rescue team and affiliated with the Scout Explorers. Teen-aged Stephanie Botko of Novato was walking up a hill when she heard some moaning. That's when she found Doris in a creek. Bradley Haas, also of Novato, another teenager was amazed that the women were able to get that far. It was hard for the young ones who were panting. One had to have ice packs and water to survive after he was overcome by the heat and exertion.

Now they had renewed hope that they would find Louise since her sister was found alive after three days. Getting Doris out of there was the big question. It was rough ground. This was an extremely difficult job for these young people. They were real heroes and heroines. They carried her to the hilltop where a Coast Guard helicopter was hovering and waiting to lift her out. It was 5:45 p.m. Friday, and she was on her way to John Muir's Medical Center in Walnut Creek and then to Doctor's Medical Center in San Pablo where she died from the exposure two days later. She had severe burns.

Neither sister had any food or drink after they started their walk. By now there were about seventy-five searchers with their dogs and a helicopter to try to locate Louise. They continued their search into the night. About 3:30 a.m. Sunday a rescue dog found her below a cliff about 220 yards away from the path. Rescuers using ropes took another two hours to get her out. She said later that she didn't realize that she had been found. She said that she was sleeping like a baby.

Debbie and her husband, Kim, deserve credit for their early untiring efforts. The family really appreciates all the hard work and caring attitudes from eleven different agencies. These are remarkable people. There was am amazing memorial service for Doris with all her siblings and almost all the searchers and helpers in that endeavor attended. Louise lived for several more years and was able to come with Debbie for another reunion with all of her family on the East Coast.

WERE THEY TERRORISTS?

Before much thought of terrorists or their hatred of Americans, Justa was aware of three men similar in appearance to the eventual perpetrators of the 9-11 crime. She was on a big plane, maybe a 747, sitting in the middle section but fairly near the back. The men were buzzing back and forth probably in Arabic. She couldn't understand, but she could see clearly the one diagonally across the aisle in front of her. He had a bag on the floor containing what resembled three thermos jugs. This man would lift one just a tiny bit and look. At first she thought he was going to take one out for a drink, but he never raised it any more than an inch or so. He seemed to be tightening or loosening or testing the top. He seemed very nervous.

She just knew that something was very strange. She finally got up and spoke to the steward who was standing in the aisle not far behind her seat. He said quietly and gently, "We are aware, and we are watching." He nodded his head toward her seat that she interpreted to mean, "My dear, this could be very serious. Please sit down. Say no more. Let us take care of it." She did just that, and the plane finished the trip and landed safely. She went on with her life and thought little about it until

9-11-01. Then she began to wonder if perhaps she and Jim had been observers in a test run for the terrorists. One of those men looked just like the one she had wondered about on that scary plane ride.

SHE HAS ASSOCIATED WITH JEWS, MUSLIMS, AND CHRISTIANS

I've told you about her wonderful first friend, Barbara, and the kindness of all of that Jewish family. Then there was a Jewish business associate of Jim's by the name of Sid Luckman. He was a star quarterback for the Chicago Bears. He was also a star businessman. He always carried a little book and pen in his right pocket. Whenever anyone made mention of a birthday, anniversary, sickness, or any way he might be helpful, it was written down immediately, and something special was done. When Wes was preparing for Eagle Scout, Sid took the time to write a personal letter and encourage him. He had another letter and gift when the job was done. When Laurie had a problem, he was there with the help. He was just a nice genuine guy.

One day Justa looked out her front door and coming down the street was a smart looking black convertible with the top down and two handsome, grinning, men in front. It was Sid and his friend, Jerry. The back was filled with the biggest, most beautiful dogwood tree one could imagine and goodness knows what else. This was Danville, Illinois, and it was trying to become **the** dogwood capital of the world. The men had driven by a florist shop and were impressed with the window display. They'd told the owner that they wanted to buy those window decorations for a friend for Mother's Day. There were told that this was the window decoration for the store and wasn't for sale. Sid assured the person that everything is for sale for a price and that this was just what he needed.

So when Justa opened the door, there these happy kind men looking like the window decoration and singing out, "*Happy Mother's Day to you*". This was a big house and had a lower and upper foyer. On that part sat a beautiful marble top table. There was a lovely carved-gold-framed mirror on the wall. On each side were green velvet chairs. Justa gave directions for the removal of one promptly, and the florist shop window decoration was placed there. It took a little adjusting, but then all agreed that it was just beautiful. It stayed right there for many months. One time when she was sick in the hospital, they showed up with the biggest bouquets of flowers she had ever seen. There were so many flowers in the room she decided that she must have died. Then she saw the biggest Hershey bar she had ever seen, and she knew she was alive, but she wasn't supposed to eat chocolate.

CHILD ABUSE CAUSES ADULT TRAUMA

There is nothing to fear but fear itself.

— Franklin DeLano Roosevelt

Justa was treated with so much love and kindness, but she still suffers from a cruelty bestowed on her as a very young child. She was playing with some other youngsters when an adult male grabbed her, opened a basement door, pushed her down onto the steps and shut the door. She was petrified and to this day suffers some claustrophobia that she attributes to that event. Perhaps the man had a mental problem or just hated children. They were all probably chattering or giggling but doing nothing to bring on that attack.

ENTRAPPED IN AN ELEVATOR

As an adult being trapped in an elevator caused something that she was later told was a heart attack. Justa and Jim had played in a late Friday afternoon golf scramble. After a good dinner with friends, they were tired and instead of walking down the steps at the El Conquistador Country Club, they decided to take the back elevator. The door shut. They pushed the down button, then every other button. They banged and shouted. Nothing happened. Her back hurt. She was really tired. She needed to go to the bathroom.

Then she realized that behind that little 12-inch door, there was probably a phone. She pulled it open, dialed the number printed there assuming it would be the elevator company. When she heard the words, "*This is the El Conquistador Country Club, Darlene Powell speaking. The office will be open at 8 a.m. Monday.*" She slid to the floor. Trapped for the weekend in this stuffy little pocket, she could hardly breath. Then she realized that if this was a real phone. They could dial 911. They did.

There was a response, but then they waited what seemed like hours. Then she remembered that all the club telephone numbers were the same except for one digit; so Jim started dialing every possibility. Finally they heard, "*El Conquistador Dining Room.*" They explained their problem. In a matter of minutes they felt the elevator shake, and they heard rumbling noises from below and voices from everywhere. When the door finally opened, there stood the chef, assistant chef, waitresses, the EMS crew, the security man from the parking lot, and other members. Justa refused help from EMS who insisted that they should take her to the hospital. The security man from the parking lot and members all offered assistance. Justa refused help, although she was shaking, and her body was cold and clammy. At a later time she was told that she had had a heart attack at sometime and that was probably when it happened. The security man said that if they had just had his number, he was right below them and could have helped them sooner.

She later learned that the telephone had not even been connected up to the day of their "entrapment."

LAUGHING'S GOOD FOR HER AND YOU

Justa thinks that laughter is such good medicine and so much better than pills, shots, or crying. Another time she had been in the hospital for what seemed an eternity as she recovered from surgery. She was tired, and she hurt. The big black nurse was exhausted from a full day of back breaking work. Now she had to give Justa a shot in the buttocks. She flipped the patient over, raised her arm high and brought the needle down hard into that skinny butt. Oh, it hurt so much, but suddenly Justa couldn't stop laughing. Whatever it was that was supposed to go into her body went all over the white uniform, sheets and everything in range. The nurse was so apologetic and embarrassed and almost in tears until she looked at Justa's face and saw that somehow this patient was hurting but forgiving and even saw humor in it. The nurse worked hard and cleaned up everything except what hit the ceiling. The service improved from that day on. Actually they became almost friends, if there is such a thing.

One day a man was bragging about the famous golfers at their course. The implication was that she had never had that experience. That's what he thought. Actually Jack Nicholas did play there one time, and he hit his ball close to her. She didn't try to explain that, of course, he was out on the fairway, and she was in the swimming pool. A little closer, and that shot could have killed her!

Another day she told this man that she and Paul Azinger had played the El Conquistador Golf Course the day before. Well, no, they weren't on the same hole, and he didn't know she was around, but the fact remains....

Laughter is the tonic, the relief, the surcease for pain.
— Charlie Chaplin

SHE WAS ALSO A MODEL AT TIMES

Model picture

Justa has done quite a bit of modeling at various places through the years. When something was too revealing or too short, and the other models were too shy, Justa agreed to wear the item. One store really wanted a swimsuit shown. She modeled the chosen suit and smiled to herself as the announcer said, "*And this can be purchased as a mastectomy suit also.*" Justa was already an octogenarian and a cancer survivor with one breast left at that time. After another style show, they were being fed in a private dining room. The waitress went around the table asking who might like iced tea. The lady on her left, *"Yes, please."* And Justa said, *"No, thank you."* As the girl passed behind Justa to offer some to the next model, some mistake was made, and suddenly, a very cold liquid was going down Justa's back from her neck all the way into her panties. Everyone was so concerned for her and that her blouse would be stained. Actually Justa had been so warm that after the initial shock, she decided that it really felt good except that she didn't like tea to drink or in her pants. Management immediately said that they would pay to have her clothes cleaned. She insisted that would not be necessary. She settled for a chocolate silk pie that was delivered to her door within the hour. It was delicious and big enough to serve her duplicate bridge group that was meeting at their home the next day. She learned later that the pie cost $17. The dry cleaning would, no doubt, be considerably cheaper.

Justa's daughter, Laurie, was talking with a friend who was due for a colonoscopy and just dreading it. Laurie knew it was far down (literally) on the list of things she wanted to do, but she gave the lady some advice. She told her, *"My mother, (that would be Justa) always said I could do anything and stand anything if I knew that there would be an end to it. In your case with that particular procedure there is always an* ***end*** *to it; so I'm sure you'll live through it."* The friend laughed, and she survived.

One day when Justa and Jim were playing golf with old friends, she hit a ball and remarked, *"I can't see where it is."* Their friend Harvey said, *"Its over there by that alligator."* She saw the log he was pointing to and knew he was teasing. He always was. She walked across the fairway, addressed her ball and swung. Just as the club head connected with the ball, the "log" raised its head and stared into Justa's eyes. Apparently he had been sleeping and wasn't quite awake. She made a hasty withdrawal.

When a neighbor, Heather, bought her new Honda, she tried car after car, and discussed it with everybody for days on end. One day Justa and Jim drove home in a new Cadillac. Heather came running out all excited. She hadn't known they were going to buy a car. Why hadn't they told her? Justa explained that they functioned differently. When they needed something, Justa made out the list. For example on this particular day, it read "bread, toilet paper, and Cadillac"; so they went out and bought bread, toilet paper, and a Cadillac. It wasn't impulse buying. They had planned it. They got a lot more done in one day, because it was usually organized. It might have read "dust the piano, call Grandma, take out the trash, and make birthday card for Matilda". People just function differently. Incidentally, that could be the car that they still have. They don't buy cars often.

Justa was part of a group called PALS, Print Artist Lovers, because they all used that program and made a lot of creative things. For example Justa made about 20 posters for a big "Pre-election party at the country club," and greeting cards, and personalized bridge tallies and score sheets. Others had many creative, unbelievable projects. They met in a nearby town for a big event to display all this and listen to speakers on different topics. The program just started when a big storm decided to join them. It thundered, and there was lightening. Suddenly the outside door opened and a woman appeared. She was soaking wet from the storm as she cried out, "*Somebody left a Cadillac trunk open, and everything is getting drenched*!" Justa knew immediately what had happened. Jim pushed a button to lock the car. He couldn't hear and didn't look. Of course, he pushed the button to open the trunk. So now he rushed out, and then of course, he too became soaked. Justa was so thankful that most of her creations were in the building and not in the trunk. They all laughed.

When they were newcomers to Bradenton, Florida they visited the Emmanuel United Methodist Church and were greeted warmly at a little social following the Sunday service. When asked if they bowled, they replied in the affirmative. When asked if they would join a league there, they replied in the negative. They already were getting so involved. But when asked if they'd be on the substitute list, they agreed. The problem was that every time they were called to sub, they already had other plans. This was embarrassing. Then one day they had a call and were asked if they were free. Justa looked at the calendar and exclaimed, "*We are. Yes, we'll be glad to.*" She hung up.

Then she noticed her right arm. It was broken and in a cast. She couldn't believe that she could forget **that** or that they would believe her when she had to call back and explain why they couldn't bowl. She humbly said, "*This isn't working. Thanks, but I think that you had better take us off the list.*" This laugh was on her.

When Justa and Jim came to parking lot and passed a man by his new car trying to take off the gas tank cover, he asked if Jim could help with this strange top. He just couldn't do it. Jim tried, and he couldn't. So without saying anything Justa (age 88) took one look, reached over and turned the top. It came right off. The man was most appreciative but obviously completely dumbfounded that this old lady could do it. As they walked off, she noticed that the man continued to stare at the old couple. She smiled. Men are a funny species.

Justa's college chum, Jan, called just out of the blue. *"Phyl, what do you think I just did?" The reply, "I haven't a clue." "Well, I just came in from a walk. I was exhausted and very hot. And so what did I do?" "Still no clue." "Well, naturally, I stripped off my clothes and stretched naked on the bed." She lived on the top floor of a high rise. "Still no clue." "Well, when I looked toward the window, what did I see?" "A window washer was looking toward me. And so what did I do?" "Well, of course, I closed my eyes. What else?"*

Justa created cards on her computer for any and all occasions. One day when she sent a get well card, she had a bouquet of flowers on it. Then across the bottom in small print she put "Please don't try to water the flowers; that would ruin the card."

Justa always takes off her tight clothes and slips into a caftan when she comes home. Therefore, she really grinned when she received the following email:

"I kept having the urge to run around the house naked. So I drank my Windex so I wouldn't streak." Anonymous

Where's the body shop?

MOVE TO FREEDOM VILLAGE

The week after they moved to the Freedom Village, they attended the first of many costume parties. They both dressed in white. Justa made a sign on the computer and hung it around her neck. It read, "Where's the body shop? We need some new parts." She had an ice pack on top of her head. She had pills for earrings. There was an eye patch over one eye. She had splints on both arms and knees. She had a heat pad on her back with the cord tied around her waist. Jim was dressed as her attendant. His sign said, "WE NEED HELP!" That's how they introduced themselves to their new neighbors. Actually they started right out participating in a lot of the many, many activities offered.

JUSTA WAS ALL WET OR AT LEAST HER CLOTHES WERE

It was January 1, 2006. They had attended a delightful New Year's Eve party and had a good sleep. This was Sunday morning, and they were dressing for church. She had put her undergarments on but had not opened her clothes closet. As she did, she saw on the floor a big mess on top of some garments. She looked up at the ceiling, and there was a big hole. The missing ceiling was the mess on the floor. Other clothes, even some on hangers, were wet. They had been out of town for about nine days. She hadn't looked at the ceiling, but there was a leak from the air conditioner. They live in Freedom Village, a nice retirement home; so she called the front desk to say that they had a problem. She called right back to say that it's not just a little problem, but a real emergency. The response was that the man would be there with 35 minutes, and he was.

Dancing New Year's Eve 2005

Fortunately she had hung her sequin New Year's party dress outside of the closet; so it was safe. She put a yardstick across the corner from one clothes rod to another. She hung a plastic pail from it under the leak so that caught the dripping water. That wonderful worker was up in there and sucked out a lot of water. She put many of the wet garments several at a time into the dryer. It was amazing that they came out as well as they did. She kept being told that management would pay for any dry cleaning, but she didn't actually want to trust some of her special clothes (accumulated around the world) to any dry cleaning establishment. The carpet was "sqwooshy". They used three bath towels at a time and blotted up as much as they could, because they did not want the other clothes to get damp and mildewed. Workmen brought a fan and came back several times checking and cleaning up. It's one way to get out of going to church, but I really think there's an easier way to do that. It seemed pretty bad until she compared it with New Orleans and Biloxi.

How lucky they are to in a retirement home where have help with their problems! They have been very happy that they made the decision to live there. They are healthier than they would be staying in a private home. There are programs to cover every phase of their lives—social, intellectual, physical, and spiritual. When they moved there, their thoughts were, "*Now we will never again have to plan or prepare a dinner. A housekeeper will clean the house and change the beds weekly. When their feeble eyes will no longer allow them to drive, transportation will be furnished.*" What more could they ask? Freedom Village had programs that would enhance their lives. She knew she could swim lengths at the pool but didn't know how much fun those silly old people could have exercising together. They use every muscle in their bodies as they grin, sing or joke at the pool three times a week.

At Fit and Trim two days per week, they stretch, use weights, and laugh some more. She line dances three days a week. There are two people certified to lead Tai Chi three times a week. This involves slow movement of arms and legs and is an aid to meditation and balance. Once a week they have "Good Morning Freedom Village". They meet together to discuss current news and thus exercise their brains. There are groans and grins and more friends. They have a wonderful bird watching group and a play reading group. After a little practice, they read in the auditorium for other residents. The chaplain manages the Sunday afternoon vesper services, Bible classes, discussions on Great Religions of the World, and also does counseling.

WE DID ALL WE COULD / WE COULDN'T SAVE HIM

It was 10:30 p.m. October 17, 2004. All Justa heard was that the phone call was from the emergency room. It came after they were retired for the night. Her first thought was that one of the children had had a car accident. Then she heard a man's voice identifying himself as a doctor and saying, "*We did all we could, but we couldn't save him.*" Then the woman's voice said that it wouldn't be necessary for them to come over. Not go to the hospital to see their only son? It was just a couple days ago that he had taken her shopping. Of course, they were dressed and there in minutes. A nurse took them across the room. She lifted a sheet, and there on a hard slab was their handsome son with his beautiful blue eyes wide open seeming to look at them. His keys were lying on his chest. It seemed to be going up and down as in breathing.

Last family picture with Wes (at both ends)

Justa cried out, "*He is alive. His eyes are open. He's breathing.*" The nurse responded, "*No, he isn't.*" She went on to explain that there was a 911 call that was responded to immediately. They found him on the floor in extreme pain. He had spent months completely restoring his condominium the way he wanted it, and now they were told that everything was a mess. He obviously had a major problem. The nurse didn't know what had happened, but there would be an autopsy. She said, "*There was no billfold*" as if that were a clue. Their imaginations went wild. Was there a break-in? Had he been attacked? Why? He was always trying to help somebody. Had he offered to help someone who then took advantage of him? Did he have an illness that they did not know about? They knew of some complications but certainly nothing this serious. This must be a nightmare. They will wake up and find it to be so. Now they were handed his keys and excused. They went back to their retirement home and to bed.

NEW CHAPLAIN

Days had gone by, but she couldn't accept this. She was just coming out of the Good Morning Freedom Village meeting when she saw a stranger in the hallway. She'd never seen this man before and didn't know why she did what she did, but she went up to him and said, "*Are you by any chance the new chaplain*?" He replied, "*Why, yes. I'm Bill Grossman, may I help you?*" She said, "*I hope so. I have a problem. I can't accept the loss of our son.*" He said, "*Would you like to talk about it?*" She hadn't been able to, but she said, "*Yes*" to this complete stranger. She went to his office. She talked, and he listened. Then he said, "*In order to have closure you will have to write an obituary and have a memorial service.*"

She wrote the obituary and sent one to a local newspaper and one to their hometown newspaper. The chaplain agreed to do the service but was going out of town for a week. He gave her his phone numbers and email address and told her to write ideas for the service as she thought of them. They made all the plans by email resulting in a beautiful memorial service honoring Wes for his constant efforts to help others. Their brothers, Glenn Miller and Wes Spalding, for whom he was named furnished the beautiful large floral arrangements created by a friend of Laurie's and placed them on either side of the podium. There was an easel on either side of this. On these were pictures of him from babyhood until his last day.

The chaplain did a wonderful job stressing Wes' achievements from Eagle Scout, to star swimmer, magician, and entertainer. He made a special point of Wes' always wanting to help somebody. His uncle, Glenn Miller, gave a eulogy. His Aunt Barbie Fisher read the eulogy that Laurie had written. Two residents kindly agreed to share their talents. Sally Stout accompanied Alice Doeden as she sang "*If I could help someone along the way*". That was so nice and made the service very special. This was held at Freedom Village, their home. Old friends and new were all kind. Each day Justa thinks that maybe her son or daughter would like this or that. But no, they are no longer here. She is in a play reading group. She had participated in several, and it was fine. Recently though she ran into a problem. She started reading a part in "Steel Magnolias" that talked about not being able to have children, buying or adopting them, the daughter's illness, childbirth, and then the death of the daughter in the play.

People often asked Justa where she got all the energy to participate in so many activities. She had been answering, "*I just do things, and that gives me more energy.*" On reading this part, she perhaps had another answer. There was a sudden realization of the deep sorrow and pain inside of her that she had been covering up with hyperactivity, smiles and laughter. Suddenly tears rolled down her cheeks for the first time, and her voice broke. She managed to finish, but the audience could barely hear her. She was facing the truth. She had wanted four children. They were able to adopt two very special ones with whom they shared their lives for all of their adulthood. Most people in retirement homes have pain. This is Justa's. Pills won't help.

Justa and Jim had purchased three condos in Bradenton. Wes is deceased, Laurie has moved to Ohio and the property has been sold. They now own no real estate anywhere. But they have had experience owning homes, condos, and a farm. Currently they are living the retirement life. This is costly, but as we get older we all need help. Residents often say, "*I thought we were supposed to be retired, and we're so busy.*" Justa replies, "*I have figured out what retired means. We were tired when we came here, but now we are tired again; so that is retired.*" When a new resident said to Justa, "*These people look old*"' Justa replied, "*That's what I thought when we moved here, but then I looked in the mirror and thought, Yep, I guess we are in the right place.*"

They have a wonderful set up when something needs fixing. Residents just phone in a "work order". Justa's first thought was, *"I should send in an order about the mirrors. They are all defective. At home we had good ones with young people in them. Every one I've checked here just has an old lady in it. They ought to be able to fix that."* It reminded her of the last time that she had her picture taken for her driver's license. She told the photographer that she wanted a picture like the one given the attractive young lady in front of her. Unfortunately she was given a photo that made her look her age! Actually they have had ceiling light bulbs, toilet seats, air conditioner filters, faucet filters, and other items replaced with a smile. I don't mean that they replaced them with smiles. I mean that they smiled when they replaced the defective items. The receptionists at the front desks are very caring and so helpful no matter what the problem. Another new resident when asked if she's happy, says, *"Oh, yes. I love it." "But how could you give up that beautiful big seven-bedroom home on the bay to come here? Why do you love it here?" "Because I don't have a house. Of course, we had help, but I had to make sure they were here and I had to supervise. No, here there are managers, housekeepers, handy men, chauffeurs, grocery shoppers, chefs, waiters and waitresses, pool maintenance, ground keepers, scheduled activities, bank, auditorium, everything. What's not to love?"* She's right, you know. We have all of that right here.

EGO BOOSTS FOR JUSTA

Bethany was retiring from the Orlando Ballet. She was the daughter of Justa's cousin, Steve. The family had invited Justa and Jim to attend performances before, but somehow this was different. Steve and his dear wife, Judy, lived in Las Cruces, New Mexico. The cousins hadn't seen each other for some time, but since Justa and Jim lived in Bradenton, Florida, Steve thought they could easily get to Orlando. They hadn't been able to do that. It was in May 2005, and Bethany would be honored for her past performances. All the family and friends were invited to the Cinderella Ballet and a party after that. Justa didn't drive any more because of her limited eyesight. Jim didn't drive that much either, but Justa said,

"Why don't we make an occasion of this? We're not taking the long trips any more. We can consider this a mini vacation. We can hire a driver, go up a day early, and stay at the Marriott across from the Performing Arts Center. We can relax and be tourists for one day. The second day we can see family, attend the performance and dinner party, and get a good night's sleep. The third day the driver can come back to Orlando and bring us home." And that's what they did. What they didn't know was that there was something special planned for Justa. As they sat in the best seats in the house the ballerina's thoughtful mother, Judy came over to them with a smile and said,

"This is just something special for you. We wanted you to know that you were Bethany's first dance teacher. We have this picture for you."

It showed Justa dancing with the little girl next to her copying the steps exactly. Apparently years ago when they were all in Colorado visiting Steve's mother, Justa's Aunt Ev, Justa had been dancing around as she still tends to do, and the child asked, "*Will you teach me how to do that?*" Of course, she did. The little girl was a natural. Bethany was honored for her years with the Orlando Ballet. After a beautiful performance, delicious dinner, and good conversation, Bethany's adoring brother presented a slide show of her dancing. It included that first "lesson". In a way it was a simple thing, but it meant a lot to that dance loving 87-year-old lady. It was the first of several "ego boosts" as Justa described them.

Bethany's first dance lesson

Backstage at Orlando Ballet

We should be generous with our compliments to others. It means so much. Bethany's family made it possible for Justa and Jim to have a lovely little holiday. Barbara Zimmerman, the driver who took care of the transportation in a professional manner made the trip possible.

On August 2005 they flew to Arlington, Virginia to celebrate Jim's niece's 35th wedding anniversary. Kathy and Frank Krogh had a wonderful gathering. Kathy confessed later that she just thought that would be a good excuse to get everybody together. It was delightful. She remembered how her parents had celebrated their 50th anniversary with Justa and Jim as the two couples were married the same year. Now the next generation was celebrating a big one. They were all included in several meals. Friends and relatives enjoyed a garden party with delicious food and a great dance band and room on a patio for them to dance. This is the couple that Justa had teased 35 years ago when she pretended that they had the hotel room in Quebec right next to the bride and groom. It wasn't held against Justa. The hostess just said they were honored that Justa and Jim were there.

Jim's youngest sister, Barbie, and her wonderful husband, Duncan, were their "caretakers" as they visited all the new memorials in Washington D. C. When they came back from a tour, Barbie told everyone in the room, *"Now I want you all to be quiet and to hear this. These two covered all the memorials and walked all over the place this hot day without*

even getting tired." When they were finally leaving at the end of the holiday, the hostess' son, Whitney, grinned and said, *"Phyl-z, I'll let you know when I get a serious girlfriend so you can plan to join us on our honeymoon."*

This family gathering was "ego boost three" for the old folks.

In September and December 2005, they visited their daughter, grandson, David, and great grandson, Braeden, in Ohio. The hostess and hosts did everything they could to entertain the visitors. A precious "ego boost four" came when the five-year-old said,

"Great-grandmother Miller is my favorite dancing partner."

Justa had become better acquainted with her nephew Eric's clan when their son, Rob, needed family history for a school project. They lived in Tennessee, Justa in Florida. His Grandpa, Wes Spalding, Justa's brother, suggested they call her. Eric's dear wife, Lynda, did all of the communicating. Phone calls and emails became more frequent as they got better acquainted. The school project was a success. When daughter, Julie, had to repeat the process, there were more questions. It turned out that Julie and Justa had numerous similarities. One email read, "*Thank you, Aunt Phyl, for the lovely detailed message. We will really enjoy that for many years. Resemblances, yes. Rob is like Grampa, and Julie is like you. You played viola. Julie does as well! Rob is and Grampa was in the marching band. Julie is and you were in the orchestra. You are all swimmers. You and Julie are the dancers."*

It was March 2006. Out of the blue, she received a call from Lynda who asked if it would be agreeable for them to come for a visit for just one day. Justa was delighted, but she didn't realize all that was in store. The school projects had included specific items some of which she was able to supply. This is an outstanding teacher who expected and received excellent work from most students. I suspect that part of the assignment could be that they must share this book with other family members but maybe not. Whether the teacher requested that or Julie or Lynda did it on their own, it was another type of "ego boost" for Justa. Julie's book is almost four inches thick and bound and is so professional looking. She carried that heavy book and brought it to show Justa and went through page by page. It's wonderful. When asked what grade she got on it, she replied, "105". They all laughed, but the teacher said that she did everything assigned perfectly and then more; so it was better than 100. What a smart teacher!

Julie Spalding showing Justa and Jim the book she made on the family history

Lynda and Justa compared notes regarding the relationship between her and her brother with the relationship of Lynda's son and daughter. The last time that Justa's brother, Wes, and his wife, Jean, visited, brother and sister swam laps and acted like two happy kids. Now he was not well enough to travel. So Lynda plugged something into something, and there were the old folks on the television screen. That was so thoughtful. Justa could see just how her brother looked as he was walking with family outside in North Carolina. That was her last view of him. He died shortly thereafter. As Lynda was doing this, she picked up her cell phone to call Eric and confirm that she was doing the correct thing with the television. That convinced Justa that Eric was in on all this planning too. They also brought other family pictures. So much of this brought back memories and made Justa feel young again. They were sharing and showing love and appreciation. When you know that the calendar says you are ancient and yet the young people can enjoy being with you and you are all having fun, that's an "ego boost". Number five? That's enough for awhile, but they are always appreciated.

I've told you just a touch of the life of one homemaker. Tell me, is she JUSTA housewife? Is anybody?

Opinion of the man who has given her love and support since that day in September, 1938 when she accepted his Beta Theta Pi fraternity pin.

"Just a housewife? Not at all. She's one special lady. Its been a real trip for 68 years, and I'm looking forward to the next ten.

Jim Miller

"Justa Mom? I don't think so!" From Laurie Miller

My brother Wes and I alternated between awe, terror, admiration, and appreciation for over 50 years. Before traveling anywhere my Mom learned enough of the language to communicate with the natives. Most Moms probably read to their children. How many try to cover the entire Great Books series? She was always teaching us something, taking us to a museum or a zoo.

And dancing? My mom can "just" hula, tango, waltz, watusi, or jitterbug with Braeden, my six year old grandson as she did with me, and my son David at that age. How many great-grandmas are still doing that? Growing up with her has never been about just any one thing. But there is one important lesson I learned from watching her. "If I set my mind to it, I can do anything." She did. I do.

Thanks mom!

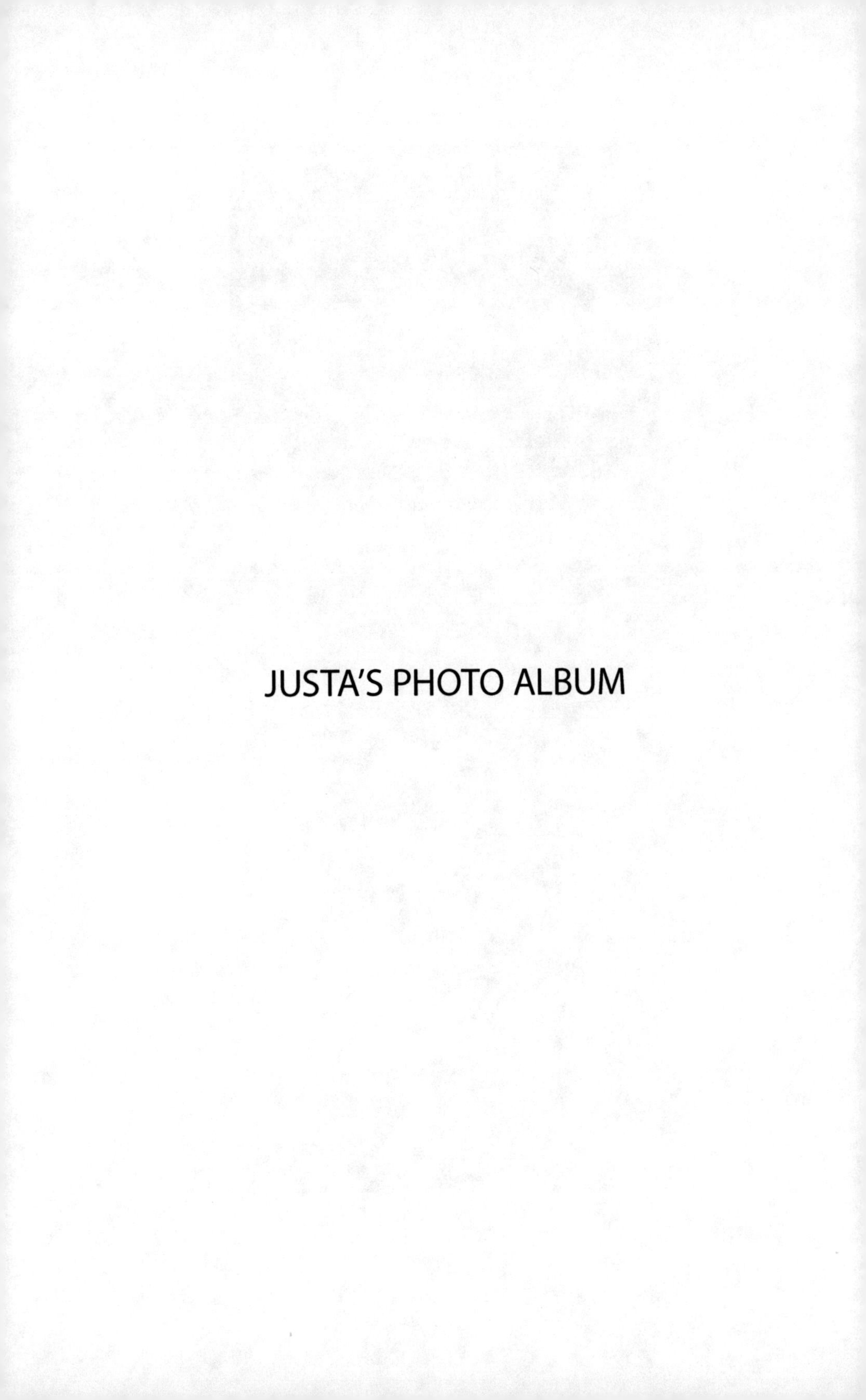

JUSTA'S PHOTO ALBUM

Algebra class mostly males

Barbie, Jim's Sister

Brother Wes, wife, and five sons skiing engineers

She played, friends sang

Coached water ballet

Justa - a diving judge for 25 years

Justa's parents 50th anniversary (1962)
Laura, Justa, John, brother Wes, Aunt Ev

Home after they worked on it

Justa hostess

Stable survived fire

Laurie's first Florida trip

Laurie ballerina

Justa and Laurie ride together

Laurie married 1968

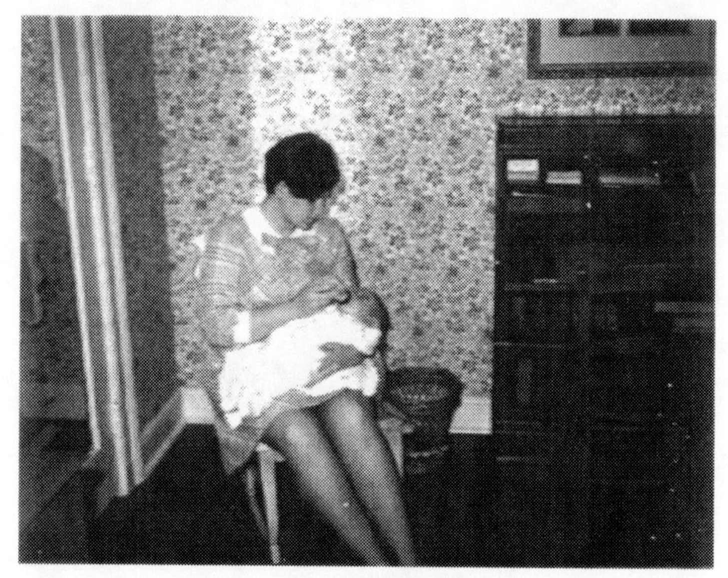

Laurie with baby David 1969

Laurie pilot

Laurie photographer

Laurie and Justa

Laurie mushing along the Iditarod Trail Alaska 1992

Chassy and David
What's going on?

Our granddaughter, Ivana Susan

Jim, Ivana with her dad Wes

Barney guards Grandpa John

Justa and Jim dancing on their 50th anniversary

Dancing with Jim (he's 91)

Justa and Jim's 50th - David emotional speech

Justa and Jim's 50th - Laurie 's speech

Wes helped prepare her 80th birthday party but won't be here for the 90th

Four generations - Laurie, David, Justa, Braeden, Jim

Wedding kimono - Japan 1972

Airport - new boots wrong feet

Dancing with Rhodesian soldier 1977

That's for the birds

Justa petting sting ray

Sailing a joy for Justa

Justa and Jim on elephant ride in India

Riding bikes to play tennis

Attacking Masai warrior

Jim petting tortoise
Galapagos Islands

Sea lion snubbing Justa
Galapagos Islands

Volunteer of the Year 1977

Justa won creative writing award Brazil 1981

Barbie visits Freedom Village

Hula at nursing home

Princess at Freedom Village

ABOUT THE AUTHOR, PHYLLIS MILLER

Who's she?

She's a funny lady and wants you to laugh. She's sad sometimes and assumes you will cry. She's had unusual experiences so hopes you will read, relax, enjoy, and maybe even learn.

For 75 years she has had articles published on inspiration, creativity, travel, antiques and "how to". She married Jim in 1941. He's a fine gentleman, a retired executive. He loves her in spite of her eccentricities or possibly because of them. They've had a life full of wonderful opportunities and adversity. She is a graduate of Rockford College and has been very active at Northwestern University where Jim earned his MBA. They both served in WW 2.

She's an adventurous world traveler, a cancer survivor, and a volunteer of the year, a loving wife, mother and grandmother. On a Rhine River cruise she was chosen Queen of the Rhine and at their retirement home, a princess. She's a vivacious almost 90-year old lady. She's interested in all people and talks to them no matter what their position, color, sex, faith, political persuasion, or nationality. When their daughter moved from Alaska and their son from California to Florida to help them in their "senility", they emailed friends, "We can't keep up with them." They almost fought over the opportunities to do nice things for their parents.

As a child she was dubbed "Little Miss Sunshine" as she roamed the neighborhood chatting with everyone. She still behaves that way. Friends and acquaintances question where she gets all the energy to do so many things. She thinks she is able to do it because she is active. She dances, swims, attends "Fit and Trim", Great Religions class, a weekly discussion group, play reading, bird watching and writes a column for Freedom Village paper.

Printed in the United States
65174LVS00005B/1-150